# The Boy Allies with the Victorious Fleets

## Robert L. Drake

The Boy Allies

With the Victorious Fleets

OR

The Fall of the German Navy

By ENSIGN ROBERT L. DRAKE

AUTHOR OF

"The Boy Allies With the Navy Series"

---

The Boy Allies

With the Navy Series

A. L. BURT COMPANY
NEW YORK

By Ensign ROBERT L. DRAKE

The Boy Allies on the North Sea Patrol
 or, Striking the First Blow at the German Fleet

The Boy Allies Under Two Flags
 or, Sweeping the Enemy from the Sea.

The Boy Allies with the Flying Squadron
 or, The Naval Raiders of the Great War.

The Boy Allies with the Terror of the Seas
 or, The Last Shot of the Submarine D-16.

The Boy Allies in the Baltic
 or, Through Fields of Ice to Aid the Czar.

The Boy Allies at Jutland
 or, The Greatest Naval Battle in History.

The Boys Allies Under the Sea
 or, The Vanishing Submarine.

The Boy Allies with Uncle Sam's Cruisers
 or, Convoying the American Army Across the Atlantic.

The Boy Allies with the Submarine D-32
 or, The Fall of the Russian Empire.

The Boy Allies with the Victorious Fleet
 or, The Fall of the German Navy.


1919
By A.L. BURT COMPANY

CONTENTS

# CHAPTER I

## ABOARD U.S.S. PLYMOUTH

"Sail at 4 a.m.," said Captain Jack Templeton of the U.S.S. Plymouth, laying down the long manila envelope marked "Secret." "Acknowledge by signal," he directed the ship's messenger, and then looked inquiringly about the wardroom table.

"Aye, aye, sir," said the first officer, Lieutenant Frank Chadwick.

"Ready at four, sir," said the engineer officer, Thomas; and left his dinner for a short trip to the engine room to push some belated repairs.

"Send a patrol ashore to round up the liberty party," continued Captain Templeton, this time addressing the junior watch officer. "Tell them to be aboard at midnight instead of eight in the morning."

"Aye, aye, sir," said the junior watch officer, and departed in haste.

There was none of the bustle and confusion aboard the U.S.S. Plymouth, at that moment lying idle in a British port, that the landsman would commonly associate with sailing orders to a great destroyer. Blowers began to hum in the fire rooms. The torpedo gunner's mates slipped detonators in the warheads and looked to the rack load of depth charges. The steward made a last trip across to the depot ship. Otherwise, things ran on very much as before.

At midnight the junior watch officer called the captain, who had turned in several hours earlier, and reported:

"Liberty party all on board, sir."

Then he turned in for a few hours' rest himself.

The junior watch was astir again at three o'clock. He routed out a sleepy crew to hoist boats and secure for sea. Seven bells struck on the Plymouth.

Captain Templeton appeared on the bridge. Lieutenant Chadwick was at his side, as were Lieutenants Shinnick and Craib, second and third officers respectively. Captain Templeton gave a command. The cable was slipped from the mooring buoy. Ports were darkened and the Plymouth slipped out. A bit inside the protection of the submarine nets, but just outside the channel, she lay to, breasting the flood tide. There she lay for almost an hour.

"Coffee for the men," said Captain Templeton.

The morning coffee was served on deck in the darkness.

Lights appeared in the distance, and presently another destroyer joined the Plymouth. Running lights of two more appeared as the clock struck 4 a.m.

Captain Templeton signalled the engine room for two-thirds speed ahead. Running lights were blanketed on the four destroyers, and the ships fell into column.

Lieutenant Chadwick felt a drop on his face. He held out a hand.

"Rain," he said briefly.

Jack—Captain Templeton—nodded.

"So much the better, Frank," he replied.

The four destroyers cleared the channel light and spread out like a fan into line formation.

"Full speed ahead!" came Jack's next command.

The Plymouth leaped ahead, as did her sister ships on either side.

"We're off," said Frank.

Away they sped in the darkness, a division of four Yankee destroyers, tearing through the Irish sea on a rainy morning; Frank knew there were four ships in line, but all he could see was his guide, a black smudge in the darkness, a few ship lengths away on his port bow. Directly she was blotted from sight by a rain squall.

"Running lights!" shouted Frank.

The lights flashed. Frank kept an eye forward. Directly he got a return flash from the ship ahead, and then picked up her shape again.

Morning dawned and still the fleet sped on. Toward noon the weather cleared. Officer and men kept their watches by regular turn during the day. At sundown the four destroyers slowed down and circled around in a slow column. The eyes of every officer watched the clock. They were watching for something. Directly it came—a line of other ships, transports filled with wounded soldiers returning to America. These must be safely convoyed to a certain point beyond the submarine zone by the Plymouth and her sister ships.

On came the transports camouflaged like zebras. The Plymouth and the other destroyers fell into line on either side of the transports.

"Full speed ahead," was Captain Templeton's signal to the engine room.

"Take a look below, Frank," said Jack to his first officer.

"Aye, aye, sir."

Frank descended a manhole in the deck. He closed the cover and secured it behind him. At the foot of the ladder was a locked door. As it opened, came a pressure on Frank's ear drums like the air-lock of a caisson. Frank threaded his way amid pumps and feed water heaters and descended still further to the furnace level.

Twenty-five knots—twenty-eight land miles an hour—was the speed of the Plymouth at that moment. It was good going.

Below, instead of dust, heat, the clatter of shovels, grimy, sweating fireman, such as the thought of the furnace room of a ship of war calls to the mind of the landsman, a watertender stood calmly watching the glow of oil jets feeding the furnace fire. Now and then he cast an eye to the gauge glasses. The vibration of the hull and the hum of the blower were the only sounds below.

For the motive power of the Plymouth was not furnished by coal. Rather, it was oil—crude petroleum—that drove the vessel along. And though oil has its advantage over coal, it has its disadvantages as well. It was Frank's first experience aboard an oil-burner, and he had not become used to it yet. He smelled oil in the smoke from the funnels, he breathed it from the oil range in the galley. His clothes gathered it from stanchions and rails.

The water tanks were flavored with the seepage from neighboring compartments. Frank drank petroleum in the water and tasted it in the soup. The butter, he thought, tasted like some queer vaseline. But Frank knew that eventually he would get used to it.

"How's she heading?" Frank asked of the chief engineer.

"All right, sir," was the reply. "Everything perfectly trim. I can get more speed if necessary."

Frank smiled.

"Let's hope it won't be necessary, chief," he replied.

He inspected the room closely for some moments, then returned to the bridge and reported to Captain Templeton.

The sea was rough, but nevertheless the speed of the flotilla was not slackened. It was the desire of Captain Petlow, in charge of the destroyer fleet, to convoy the transports beyond the danger point at the earliest possible moment.

The Plymouth lurched up on top of a crest, then dived head-first into the trough. On the bridge the heave and pitch of the vessel was felt subconsciously, but the eyes and minds of the officers were busied with other things. At every touch of the helm the vessel vibrated heavily.

Eight bells struck.

"Twelve o'clock," said Frank. "Time to eat."

The bridge was turned over to the second officer, and Frank and Jack went below.

"Eat is right, Frank," said Jack as they sat down. "We can't dine in this weather."

It was true. The rolling boards, well enough for easy weather, proved a mockery in a sea like the one that raged now. Butter balls, meat and vegetables shot from plates and went sailing about. It was necessary to drink soup from teacups and such solid foods as Jack and Frank put into their stomachs was only what they succeeded in grabbing as they leaped about on the table.

The two returned on deck.

The day passed quietly. No submarines were sighted, and at last the flotilla reached the point where the destroyers were to leave the homeward bound transports to pursue their voyage alone. The transports soon grew indistinguishable, almost, in the semi-darkness. The senior naval officer aboard the Plymouth hoisted signal flags.

"Bon Voyage," they read.

Through a glass Jack read the reply.

"Thank you for your good work. Best of luck."

From the S.N.O. (senior naval officer) came another message. Frank picked it up.

"Set course 188 degrees. Keep lookout for inbound transports to be convoyed. Ten ships."

Again the destroyer swung into line. It was almost seven o'clock—after dark—when the lookout aboard the Plymouth reported:

"Smoke ahead!"

Instantly all was activity aboard the destroyers. Directly, through his glass, Jack sighted nine rusty, English tramp steamers, of perhaps eight thousand tons, and a big liner auxiliary flying the Royal Navy ensign.

Under the protection of the destroyers, the ships made for an English port. The night passed quietly. With the coming of morning, the flotilla was divided. The Plymouth stood by to protect the big liner, while the other three destroyers and the tramp steamers moved away toward the east.

"This destroyer game is no better than driving a taxi," Frank protested to Jack on the bridge that afternoon. You never see anything. I'd like to get ashore for a change. I've steamed sixty thousand miles since last May and what have I seen? Three ports, besides six days' leave in London."

"You had plenty of time ashore before that," replied Jack.

"Maybe I did. But I'd like to have some more. Besides, this isn't very exciting business."

Night fell again, and still nothing had happened to break the quiet monotony of the trip. Lights of trawlers flashed up ahead. Interest on the bridge picked up.

"Object off the port bow," called the lookout.

"Looks like a periscope," reported the quartermaster.

Frank snapped his binoculars on a bobbing black spar.

"Buoy and fishnet," he decided after a quick scrutiny.

Frank kept the late watch that night. At 4 a.m. he turned in. At five he climbed hastily from his bunk at the jingle of general alarm, and reached the bridge on the run in time to see the exchange of recognition signals with a British man-o'-war, which vessel had run into a submarine while the latter was on the surface in a fog. The warship had just rammed the U-boat.

"Can we help you?" Frank called across the water.

"Thanks. Drop a few depth charges," was the reply.

This was done, but nothing came of it Frank returned to his bunk.

"Pretty slow life, this, if you ask me," he told himself.

He went back to sleep.

## CHAPTER II

## THE BOY CAPTAIN AND HIS LIEUTENANT

The U.S.S. Plymouth was Jack Templeton's first command. He had been elevated to the rank of captain only a few weeks before. Naturally he was not a little proud of his vessel. When Jack was given his ship, it was only natural, too, that Frank Chadwick, who had been his associate and chum through all the days of the great war, should become Jack's first officer.

In spite of the fact that Jack's rating as captain was in the British navy, he was at this moment in command of an American vessel. This came about through a queer combination of circumstances.

The American commander of the Plymouth had been taken suddenly ill. At almost the same time the Plymouth had been ordered to proceed from Dover to Liverpool to join other American vessels. Almost on the eve of departure, the first officer also was taken ill. It was to him the command naturally would have fallen in the captain's absence. The second officer was on leave of absence. Thus, without a skipper, the Plymouth could not have sailed.

Jack and Frank had recently returned with a British convoy from America. They were in Dover at the time. From his sick bed in a hospital, the captain of the Plymouth had appealed to the British naval authorities. In spite of the fact that he was in no condition to leave when he received his orders, he did not wish to deny his crew the privilege of seeing active service, which the call to Liverpool, he knew, meant.

The captain's appeal had been turned over to Lord Hastings, now connected prominently with the British admiralty. Lord Hastings, in the early days of the war, had been the commander under whom Jack and Frank had served. In fact, the lads were visiting the temporary quarters of Lord Hastings in Dover when the appeal was received from the commander of the Plymouth.

"How would you like to tackle this job, Jack?" Lord Hastings asked.

"I'd like it," the lad replied, "if you think I can do it, sir."

"Of course you can do it," was Lord Hastings' prompt reply. "I haven't sailed with you almost four years for nothing."

"You mean, sir," replied Jack with a smile, "that I haven't sailed with you that long for nothing."

"That's more like it, Jack," put in Frank laughingly. "I've learned a few things from Lord Hastings myself."

"It is hardly probable," continued Lord Hastings, "that your promotion has been unearned, Jack. No, I believe you can fill the bill."

"In that case, I shall be glad to take command of the Plymouth temporarily, sir."

"And how about me?" Frank wanted to know. "Where do I come in, sir?"

"Why," said Lord Hastings, "I have no doubt it can be arranged so you can go along as first officer. I understand the first officer of the Plymouth is also under the weather."

"But isn't all this a bit irregular, sir?" Jack asked.

"Very much so," was Lord Hastings' reply. "At the same time, many precedents are being broken every day, and I can see no reason why two British officers cannot lend their services to an ally if they are asked to do so."

"It is a little different with me, sir," said Frank. I'm an American."

"All the same," said Lord Hastings, "you're a British naval officer, no matter what your nativity."

"That's true, too, sir," Frank agreed. "I haven't thought of it in just that way."

"Well," said Lord Hastings, "I shall report then that Captain Templeton and First Lieutenant Chadwick will go aboard the Plymouth this evening."

"Very well, sir," said Jack.

This is the reason then that Jack and Frank found themselves aboard an American destroyer in the Irish sea.

Frank Chadwick, as we have seen, was an American. He had been in Italy with his father when the great war began. He had been shanghaied in Naples soon after Germany's declaration of war on France. When he came to his senses he found that his captors were a band of mutinous sailors. Aboard the vessel he found a second prisoner, who turned out to be a member of the British secret service.

Frank met Jack Templeton, a British youth, aboard the schooner. Jack came aboard in a peculiar way.

The schooner, in control of the mutineers, had put into a north African port for provisions. Now it chanced that the store where the mutineers sought to buy provisions was conducted by Jack. The lad was absent when the supplies were purchased and returned a few moments later to find that the mutineers had departed without making payment.

Jack's anger bubbled over. He put off for the schooner in a small boat. Aboard, the chief of the mutineers refused the demand for payment. A fight ensued. Jack, facing heavy odds, sought refuge in the hold of the vessel, where he was made a prisoner.

During the night Jack was able to force his way from the hold into the cabin where Frank and the British secret service agent were held captives. He released them, and joining forces, the three were able to overcome the mutineers and make themselves masters of the ship.

Now Jack Templeton was an experienced seaman and knew more than the rudiments of navigation. Under his direction the schooner returned to the little African port that he called home. There the three erstwhile prisoners left the ship to the mutineers.

Later, through the good offices of the British secret service, Frank and Jack made the acquaintance of Lord Hastings, also in the diplomatic service. They were able to render some service to the latter and later accompanied him to his home in London. There, at their request, Lord Hastings, who in the meantime had been given command of a ship of war, had them attached to his ship with the rank of midshipmen.

Both Jack and Frank had risen swiftly in the British service. They had seen active service in all quarters of the globe and had fought under many flags.

Under Lord Hastings' command they had been with the British fleet in the North Sea when it struck the first decisive blow against the Germans just off Helgoland. Later they were found under the Tricolor of France and with the Italians in the Adriatic. With the British fleet again when it sallied forth to clear the seven seas of enemy vessels, they had traversed the Atlantic, the Pacific and the Indian oceans. It had been their fortune, too, to see considerable land fighting. They had been with the Anglo-Japanese forces in the east and had conducted raiding parties in some of the German colonial possessions.

Several times they had successfully run the blockade in the Kiel canal, passing through the narrow straits in submarines just out of reach of the foe. In Russia, they had, early in the war, lent invaluable assistance to the Czar; and more lately, they had been in the eastern monarchy when Czar Nicholas had been forced to renounce his throne.

Once since the war began they had been to America. This was shortly after the United States entered the war. They were ordered to the North Atlantic in order to help the American authorities snare a German commerce raider which, in some unaccountable manner, had run the British blockade in the North sea, and was wreaking havoc with allied shipping. Later they went to New York, and then returned to Europe with a combined British-American convoy for the first expeditionary force to cross the seas.

In temperament and disposition Jack and Frank were as unlike as one could conceive. Jack, big for his age, broad-shouldered and strong, was always cool and collected. Frank, on the other hand, was of a more fiery nature, easily angered and often rash and reckless.

Jack's steadying influence had often kept the two out of trouble, or brought them through safely when they were in difficulties.

Both lads spoke French and German fluently and each had a smattering of Italian. Also, as the result of several trips to Russia, they had a few words of the Russian tongue at their command.

In physical strength, Jack excelled Frank by far, although the latter was by no means a weakling. On the other hand again, Frank was a crack shot with either rifle or revolver; in fact, he was such an excellent marksman as to cause his chum no little degree of envy. Then, too, both lads were proficient in the art of self defense and both had learned to hold their own with the sword.

Up to the time this story opens the combined allied fleets had succeeded in keeping the Germans bottled up in the strong fortress of Helgoland. True, the enemy several times had sallied forth in few numbers, apparently seeking to run the blockade in an effort to prey upon allied merchant ships. But every time they had offered battle they had received the worst of it. They had been staggered with a terrible defeat at Jutland almost a year before this story opens, and since that time had not ventured forth.

But even now, in the security of their hiding places, the Germans were meditating a bold stroke. Submarines were being coaled and victualed in preparation for a dash across the Atlantic. Already, one enemy submarine—a merchantman—had passed the allied ships blocking the English channel and had crossed to America and returned. Some months later, a U-Boat of the war type had followed suit. A cordon of ally ships had been thrown around American ports to snare this venturesome submarine on its return, but it had eluded them and returned safely to its home port.

But soon—very soon, indeed—German undersea craft were to strike a more severe blow at allied shipping, carrying, for the moment, the war in all its horrors to the very door of America. While the United States was arming and equipping its millions to send across the sea to destroy the kaiser and German militarism, these enemy undersea craft were crossing the Atlantic determined to reap a rich harvest upon American, allied and neutral shipping off the American coast.

And the blow was to be delivered without warning — almost.

When the U.S.S. Plymouth, under Jack's command, returned to Liverpool, the captain of the vessel, having somewhat recovered, came aboard and relieved Jack of command.

"I'm obliged for your services, Captain," he said, "but I'll take charge of the old scow again myself, with your leave."

Jack and Frank went ashore, where, at their hotel, they received a brief telegram from Lord Hastings. It read as follows:

"Return to Dover at once. Important."

"Now I wonder what is up," said Frank after reading the message.

"The simplest way to find out," replied Jack, "is to go and see."

## CHAPTER III

## OFF FOR AMERICA

"Then everything went first rate your first trip, Captain?" questioned Lord Hastings.

"First rate, sir," Jack replied.

The lads were back in Dover where, the first thing after their arrival, they sought an audience with their former commander.

"Yes, sir," Frank agreed, "Jack makes an A-1 captain."

"I'm glad to hear it," was Lord Hastings' comment. "I've other work in hand and I wouldn't want to trust it to a man who is nervous under fire."

"But we were not under fire this time, sir," said Jack.

"You mustn't always take me literally, Jack," smiled Lord Hastings. "It was your first venture in your present rank and you acquitted yourself creditably. That is what I meant."

"And what is the other venture, sir?" Frank asked eagerly.

"There you go again, Frank," said Lord Hastings. "How many times have I told you that you must restrain your impatience."

Frank was abashed.

"Your warnings don't seem to do much good, I'll admit, sir. Nevertheless, I'll try to do better."

"See that you do," returned Lord Hastings gravely. "Nothing was ever gained by too great impatience. Remember that."

"I'll try, sir."

"Very well. Then I shall acquaint you with the nature of the work in hand."

The boys listened intently to Lord Hastings' next words.

"As you know," His Lordship began, "the seas have virtually been cleared of all enemy ships. All German merchant vessels have been captured or sunk. What few raiders that preyed on our commerce for a time have been put out of business."

"Yes, sir," said Jack. "Our merchant vessels no longer have anything to fear from the foe."

"They shouldn't, that's true enough," replied Lord Hastings.

"You mean they have, sir?" asked Jack, incredulously.

Lord Hastings nodded.

"I do," he admitted gravely. "Particularly shipping on the other side of the Atlantic."

"America, sir?"

"Exactly."

"But surely," Frank put in, "surely our blockade is tight enough to prevent the enemy from breaking through."

"We have not yet found means," replied Lord Hastings, "of effectually blockading the submarine."

"Oh, I see," said Frank. "You mean that the Germans plan to open a submarine campaign upon allied shipping in American waters."

"Such is my information," declared Lord Hastings.

"And," said Jack, "you wish us to cross the Atlantic and take a hand in the game of taming the U-Boats, sir."

"Such is my idea," Lord Hastings admitted. "Let me explain. My information is not authentic, but nevertheless, knowing the Germans as I do, I am tempted to credit it."

"Then why not warn the United States, sir?" asked Frank. "There are enough American ships of war off the coast to deal effectually with all the submarines the Germans can get across."

"So I would," was Lord Hastings' reply, "but for the fact that some officials of the admiralty are opposed to it."

"Opposed?" exclaimed Jack. "And why, sir?"

"Because they labor under the delusion that such a warning would throw the people of the United States into a panic and would prevent the sending of additional troops to France."

"What a fool idea! By George!" exclaimed Frank, "what do they think the American people are made of?"

"You'll have to ask them," was Lord Hastings' answer to this question. "For my own part, I feel that it is hardly fair to keep this information from the American authorities."

"I should say it isn't fair," declared Frank.

"I agree with you," said Jack. "But just where do Frank and I come in, sir?"

"I'll make that plain to you very quickly," replied Lord Hastings.

He drew a paper from his pocket and passed it to Jack.

"Here," he said, "is your commission as captain of H.M.S. Brigadier." He passed a second paper to Frank. "This," he continued, "is your commission as first officer of the same vessel. Now, through channels known only to myself, I have induced the admiralty to send you to America with certain papers for Secretary Daniels of the navy department. At the same time, I have other personal papers which I shall have you deliver to the secretary of the navy for me. These will acquaint him with the facts I have just laid before you."

"I see, sir," said Jack. "But, if you will pardon my asking, what will happen to you sir should it be found out you have acted contrary to the wishes of the admiralty majority?"

Lord Hastings shrugged his shoulders disdainfully.

"What's the difference?" he wanted to know. "Our allies must be warned."

"I agree with you, sir," declared Jack.

"And I, sir," said Frank.

"It is possible," said Lord Hastings, "that should I take the matter up with the King or with the war ministry I might get action; but that would take time, and I want this message delivered at the earliest possible moment. Should I entrust it to the cables, under the circumstances, there is nothing certain of its arrival."

"I see, sir," said Jack. "Then you may be sure that I shall deliver the message personally to Secretary Daniels."

"It is well," said Lord Hastings. "I knew I could depend upon you boys."

"Always, sir," replied Jack simply.

"Then be off with you," said Lord Hastings, rising. "You can go aboard your ship to-night. Here is the message I wish delivered to the American secretary of the navy," and he passed a second paper to Jack. "The admiralty message you are to take will probably reach you some time in the morning, together with your sailing orders."

Lord Hastings extended his hand.

"Good-bye and good luck," he said.

Jack and Frank shook hands with him and took their departure.

"I'll be glad to get back to America if only for a short time," said Frank, as they walked toward the water front.

"I won't mind another look at the United States myself," Jack declared. "It looks like a pretty good country to me, from what I saw of it last trip. Almost as good as England, I guess."

"Almost?" repeated Frank. "Say, let me tell you something. The United States is the greatest country under the sun and don't you forget it. You Johnny Bulls seem to think that England is the only spot on the map."

"Well," returned Jack with a smile, "it strikes me that you boast considerably about your own land."

Frank's face reddened a trifle.

"Maybe I do," he admitted, "but it's worth it."

"So is England," said Jack quietly.

"By George! So it is, Jack," said Frank. "Maybe it is a fact that I talk too much sometimes."

"No 'maybes' about it," declared Jack. "It's just a plain fact."

"Look here," said Frank, somewhat nettled, "you may be my boss aboard ship, but right now, with no witnesses present to hear what I say, I'll say what I like."

"Come, come, now," said Jack with a smile, "don't get all out of humor just because I joke you a little bit."

Frank grinned.

"Well, then don't always thinks I'm angry just because I make a hot reply," he said.

Jack let it go at that.

"Well, here we are at the water front," he said a few moments later, "and if I'm not mistaken that's the Brigadier about a hundred yards off shore there."

"That's the Brigadier, all right," said Frank, "I can see her name forward even at this distance. By George! but the camouflage artists have certainly done a good job on her."

"So they have," Jack agreed. "But we may as well go aboard."

They commandeered a small boat and rowed rapidly to the Brigadier. Jack swung himself up on deck and Frank climbed up behind him.

A young lieutenant greeted Jack respectfully after a quick glance at the latter's bars.

"What can I do for you, sir?" he asked.

"You may go below and tell the engineer to get steam up immediately," replied Jack. "We may not sail before morning, but I may desire to leave before."

"Very well, sir," replied the young officer, "but may I ask who you are, sir?"

"Certainly," replied Jack, "I'm the commander of this ship, Captain Templeton. This is Mr. Chadwick, my first officer. What is your name, sir?"

"Hetherton, sir, second officer of the Brigadier."

"Very good, Lieutenant. You shall stay on here as second officer until further notice. Now below with you."

Lieutenant Hetherton disappeared.

"I guess he won't ask many more questions," said Frank grimly.

"Perhaps not," said Jack. "Now, Mr. Chadwick, will you be so kind as to take the deck while I go to my cabin."

Frank seemed about to remark upon Jack's sudden change in manner. Then he thought better of it and walked off, grumbling to himself.

"Wonder what he's in such an all-fired rush about? He's not wasting any time, that's sure."

He took the deck. Ten minutes later Lieutenant Hetherton reported to him, saluting at the same time.

"Engineer says he'll have steam up in two hours, sir."

"Very well," replied Frank, returning the salute. "Will you kindly take the deck, Lieutenant Hetherton? I'm going below."

Lieutenant Hetherton took the deck, and thus relieved, Frank went below and sought out Jack's cabin.

"Now," he said, "I'll find out what all this rush is about."

Without the formality of a knock, he went in.

## CHAPTER IV

## THE START

Inside Jack's cabin, Frank found his commander and chum engaged in conversation with the engineer officer, who had sought his new commander immediately after giving instructions below. He saluted Frank as the lad entered.

"My first officer, Lieutenant Chadwick, Mr. Winslow," Jack introduced them. "I am sure you will get along together."

"So am I, sir," agreed the engineer. "And when shall we be moving, sir?"

"I can't say, exactly," replied Jack. "Probably not before morning, but I wish to be ready to leave on a moment's notice."

"Very well, sir," said the engineer, "As I said before, I'll have steam up in two hours."

"Do so, sir."

The engineer saluted and left Jack's cabin.

Jack turned to Frank.

"Now," he said, "what are you doing here? I thought I left you to take the deck?"

"I turned the deck over to Hetherton," replied Frank with a grin. "I wanted to find out what all this rush is about?"

"Don't you know it's bad form to ask questions of your commander?" Jack said severely.

"Maybe it is," Frank agreed, "but I just wanted to find out."

"Well, I wouldn't do it in front of any of the other officers or the men," said Jack. "It's bad for the ship's discipline. However, I'll tell you, I just wanted to have things ready, that's all. Come, we'll go on deck."

They ascended to the bridge. Jack addressed Lieutenant Hetherton.

"Pipe all hands on deck for inspection, Lieutenant," he ordered.

Lieutenant Hetherton passed the word. A moment later men came tumbling up the companion way and fell into line aft. Jack and Frank walked forward to look them over. Jack addressed a few words to the men.

"I've just taken over command of the Brigadier," he said. "To-morrow morning, or sooner, we shall sail, our destination temporarily to be known only to myself. I believe that I may safely promise you some action before many days have passed."

A hearty British cheer swept the ship.

"Hurrah!" cried the men.

A few moments later Jack dismissed them. Then the officers returned to the bridge, where Jack told off the watches.

"Now," he said, "I'll have to look over the ship."

Frank accompanied him on his tour of inspection. They found everything absolutely clean and ship-shape. The muzzles of the big guns were shining brightly beneath their coat of polish. After the inspection, Jack and Frank went below for a look at the ship's papers.

The Brigadier was a small destroyer, not more than 200 feet long. It had a complement of 250 men, officers and crew; carried two batteries of 9-inch guns in turrets forward and aft and was equipped with three 2-inch torpedo tubes. It was not one of the latest of British destroyers, but still it was modern in many respects.

"A good ship," said Jack, after a careful examination of the papers. "As to speed, we should get twenty-three knots on a pinch. Her fighting equipment is excellent, everything is spick and span, and I was impressed with the officers and crew. Yes, she is a good ship."

"And you're the boss of the whole ranch, Jack," said Frank. "Think of it. Less than four years ago you knew nothing at all of naval tactics, and now you're in command of a British destroyer. By George! I wouldn't mind having your job myself."

Jack smiled.

"Never mind," he said. "You'll get yours some day. I've just been more fortunate, that's all. Besides, I knew something of navigation before you did, and while you have mastered it now, I had a long start."

"That's true enough," Frank admitted, "but at the same time you are considerably more fit for the job than I am. Another thing. I don't know that I would trade my berth here for a command of a ship."

Jack looked his surprise.

"Why?" he asked.

"Because it would separate us," was Frank's reply. "We've been together now since the war began, almost. I hope that we may see it through together."

"Here, too," declared the commander of the Brigadier, "but at the same time you should not let a matter of friendship stand between you and what may be your big opportunity."

"Oh, I'd probably take the job if it were offered me," said Frank. "I'm just hoping the offer will not be made; that's all."

The lads conversed for some moments longer. Then Frank looked at his watch.

"My watch," he said quietly. "I'll be going on deck."

"Right," said Jack. "Call me if anything happens."

"Yes, sir," said Frank, saluting his commander gravely.

Jack grinned.

"By Jove! It seems funny to have you talk like that to me," he said. "At the same time I suppose it must be done for the sake of discipline. However, it is not necessary in private."

"Nevertheless," said Frank, "I had better stick to it or I'm liable to forget in public some time."

"Well, maybe you're right," said Jack.

Frank turned on his heel and went on deck, where he relieved Lieutenant Hetherton, who had been on watch.

"Nothing to report, sir," said Lieutenant Hetherton, saluting.

"Very well, sir," was Frank's reply, as he, too, saluted.

It was after midnight, and Frank's watch was nearing its end when the lookout on the port side called:

"Boat off the port bow, sir."

Frank advanced to the rail. A moment later there was a hail from the water.

"What ship is that?'

"His Majesty's Ship Brigadier," Frank called back.

"I'm coming aboard you," said the voice from the darkness. "Lower a ladder."

Frank gave the necessary command. A few moments later a man attired in the uniform of a British captain came over the side. He approached Frank, who was barely visible in the darkness.

"Captain Templeton?" he asked.

"No, sir. I'm Lieutenant Chadwick. A moment, sir, and I'll call the captain."

"If you please," said the visitor.

Frank passed the word for the quartermaster, who arrived within a few moments.

"Call Captain Templeton," Frank directed.

Jack arrived on deck a few moments later and exchanged greetings with his visitor. The latter produced a packet of papers.

"From the admiralty," he said. "You will know what to do with them."

Jack took the papers and stowed them in his pocket.

"Yes, sir," he said.

"That is all, then," said the visitor. "I shall be going."

He stepped to the side of the vessel and disappeared.

"This means," said Jack, after the other had gone, "that we can sail any time now."

"Then why not at once?" asked Frank.

"You anticipated me," replied Jack. "Will you kindly pipe all hands on deck, Mr. Chadwick?"

Frank passed the word.

Sleepy men came tumbling from their bunks below. All became bustle and hurry aboard the Brigadier. Jack himself took the bridge. Frank stood beside him. Other officers took their places.

"Man the guns!" came Jack's order.

It was the lad's intention to overlook nothing that would protect the ship should it encounter an enemy submarine en route, and, as the lad knew, it was just as possible they would encounter one in the English Channel as elsewhere.

For, despite all precautions taken by British naval authorities, enemy submarines more than once had crept through the channel, once penetrating Dover harbor itself, where they had wreaked considerable damage before being driven away by British destroyers and submarine chasers.

A few moments later Jack signaled the engine room.

"Half speed ahead."

Slowly the Brigadier slipped from her anchorage and moved through the still waters of the harbor. Directly she pushed her nose into the channel, then headed east.

"Full speed ahead!" Jack signaled the engine room.

The Brigadier leaped forward.

"Better turn in, Jack," said Frank. "It's Thompson's watch."

"No, I'll stick until we reach the Atlantic," returned Jack.

"Then I'll stick along," said Frank.

This they did.

It was hours later when the Brigadier ran clear of the channel and breasted the heavy swell of the Atlantic. Jack spoke to Thompson, the third officer.

"I'm going to turn in," he said. "If anything happens, call me at once."

"Very well, sir," was the third officer's reply.

He saluted briefly. Jack and Frank went below.

"Come in a moment before you turn in, if you wish," Jack said to Frank.

"May as well," replied the latter. "I don't feel like turning in for an hour yet."

"Well, you can't keep me out of bed that long," declared Jack. "I've got to be stirring before you go on watch again. But I thought we might talk a few moments."

Nevertheless, it was an hour later that Frank went to his own cabin. He turned in at once and was soon fast asleep.

On the other hand, sleep did not come to Jack so soon. For an hour or more he lay in his bunk, reviewing the events of the past and his responsibilities of the present.

"It's a big job I have now," he told himself. "I hope I can carry it through successfully."

But he didn't have the slightest doubt that he could. Jack's one best characteristic was absolute confidence in himself.

## CHAPTER V

## A RESCUE

H.M.S. Brigadier was steaming steadily along at a speed of twenty knots. Jack himself held the bridge. Frank and Lieutenant Hetherton, who stood nearby, were discussing the sinking several days before of a large allied transport by a German submarine in the Irish sea.

"She was sunk without warning, the same as usual," said Hetherton.

"The Germans never give warning any more," replied Frank, "Of course, the reason is obvious enough. To give warning it would be necessary for the submarine to come to the surface, in which case the merchant ship might be able to place a shell aboard the U-Boat before she could submerge again. So to take time to give warning would be a disadvantage to the submarine."

"At the same time," said Hetherton, "it's an act of barbarism to sink a big ship without giving passengers and crew a word of warning."

"Oh, I'm not defending the German system," declared Frank. "I am just giving you what I believe is the German viewpoint."

"Nevertheless," said Hetherton, "it's about time such activities were stopped."

"It certainly is. But it seems that the U-Boats are growing bolder each day."

"It wouldn't surprise me," declared Lieutenant Hetherton, "to hear almost any day that U-Boats had crossed the Atlantic to prey on shipping in American waters."

Frank looked at the second officer sharply. He was sure that Jack had not divulged the real reason for their present voyage, and he had said nothing about the matter himself.

"Just a chance remark, I guess," Frank told himself. Aloud he said: "I hardly think it will come to that."

"I hope not," replied Hetherton, "but you never can tell, you know."

"That's true enough, too," Frank agreed, "but at the same — "

He broke off suddenly as he caught the sharp hail of the forward lookout.

"Ship in distress off the port bow, sir," came the cry.

Jack was at once called to the deck.

Instantly Frank and Lieutenant Hetherton sprang to Jack's side. At almost the same moment the radio operator emerged from below on the run.

"Message, sir," he exclaimed, and thrust a piece of paper in Jack's hand. Jack read it quickly. It ran like this:

"Merchant steamer Hazelton, eight thousand tons, New York to Liverpool with munitions and supplies, torpedoed by submarine. Sinking. Help."

"Did you get her position?" demanded Jack of the wireless operator.

"No, sir. The wireless failed before he could give it."

"Don't you think it may be the vessel ahead, sir?" asked Lieutenant Hetherton.

"Can't tell," was Jack's reply. "It may be, in which case there are probably more submarines about. Clear ship for action, Mr. Chadwick."

No sooner said than done.

Frank and others of the ship's officers darted hither and yon, making sure that everything was in readiness. At the guns, the gunners grinned cheerfully. Frank approached the battery in the forward turret.

"All right?" he asked.

"O.K., sir," replied the officer in command of the gun crew. "Show us a submarine, that's all we ask."

"There are probably a dozen or so about here some place," returned Frank. "Keep your eyes peeled and don't wait an order to fire if you see anything that looks like one."

"Right, sir."

The officer turned to his men with a sharp command.

Frank continued his inspection of the ship as the Brigadier dashed toward the vessel in distress, probably ten miles ahead.

Every man aboard the Brigadier was on the alert as the destroyer plowed swiftly through the water. It was possible, of course, that the submarines had made off after attacking the vessel, but there was always the possibility that some were still lurking in the neighborhood.

"Can't be too careful," Jack told himself.

Fifteen minutes later, the lookout was able to make out more clearly the ship ahead of them.

"Steamer Hazelton," he called to the quartermaster, who reported to Jack.

"Same vessel that sent the wireless, Frank," was Jack's comment. "We will have to look sharp. It's more than an even bet that some of those undersea sharks are watching for a ship to come to the rescue so they can have a shot at her also."

"We're ready for 'em," said Frank significantly.

"All right," said Jack. "In the meantime we'll stand by the Hazelton and see if we can lend a hand."

As the Brigadier drew closer those on deck could see signs of confusion aboard the Hazelton. Then there arose a large cloud of smoke that for a moment hid the Hazelton from view. This was followed by a loud explosion.

When the smoke cleared away, the water nearby was filled with struggling figures.

"Lower the boats," shouted Jack.

Instantly men sprang to obey the command, while others of the British tars still stood quietly behind their guns, their eyes scanning the sea.

Aboard the Hazelton, the crew, or what remained of the crew, were attempting to lower lifeboats. Directly one was lowered safely, and loaded to the guards with human freight. A second and a third were lowered safely, and put off toward the Brigadier.

In the meantime, lifeboats from the destroyer had darted in among the struggling figures and willing hands were lifting the victims to safety. Then these, in turn, started back to the destroyer.

"I guess they're all off," said Frank to Jack.

"I hope so," was Jack's reply. "If I am not mistaken, there are women among the survivors."

"By George! I thought I saw some myself," was Frank's answer.

Suddenly there was a crash as the forward turret guns aboard the Brigadier burst into action. Looking ahead, Jack gave a startled cry, and no wonder.

For, from beneath the water, appeared a periscope and then the long low outline of a German submarine came into view.

Again the Brigadier's guns crashed, but the shells did not strike home.

Before the destroyer could fire again, a gun appeared as if by magic on the submarine's deck, and a hail of bullets was poured into the first of the nearby lifeboats. At the same time the U-Boat launched a torpedo at the Brigadier.

Jack gave a cry of horror at the predicament of those in the small boats. But he did not lose his head, and at the same time maneuvered his ship out of the path of the torpedo.

Came a hail from the lookout aft.

"Submarine off the stern, sir!"

At the same moment the battery in the Brigadier's turret aft burst into action.

"Forward with you, Mr. Chadwick," cried Jack, "and see if you can't get better results there. The men seem to have lost their nerve."

Frank sprang forward. Jack's words were true. It appeared that the crew in the forward turret were so anxious to sink the first submarine that they had not taken time to find the range.

"Cease firing!" shouted Frank as he sprang into the turret.

The order was obeyed, but there came a grumble from the men at what they deemed such a strange command under the circumstances.

"I thought you fellows were gunners," said Frank angrily. "Smith, get the range."

Smith did so, and announced it a moment later.

"Now," said Frank, "get your aim, men."

No longer was there confusion in the forward turret. The guns were trained carefully.

"Ready," cried Frank. "Fire!"

"Crash!"

A moment and there was a loud cheer from the crew. The German submarine seemed to leap high from the water, and then fell back in a dozen pieces.

Frank wasted no further time on the first submarine. Leaving the forward turret, he dashed aft to where other guns were firing on the second submarine. Meantime Jack, perfectly cool on the bridge, had maneuvered his vessel out of the way of several torpedoes from the second U-Boat. But, as he very well knew, this combat must be brought to a quick end or one of the torpedoes was likely to find its mark.

From the deck of the second submarine, a hail of fire from a machine gun was still being poured into the helpless lifeboats. What execution had been done Jack had no means of telling at the moment, but he knew there must have been some casualties.

"The brutes!" he muttered.

The duel between the submarine and the destroyer still raged. It appeared that the commander of the submarine was a capable officer, for he had succeeded in keeping his vessel from being struck by a shell from the Brigadier.

In the aft turret of the Brigadier the British tars were sweating and muttering imprecations at their inability to put a shell aboard the enemy.

"Here," said Frank, "let me get at that gun."

The crew stepped aside and the lad sighted the weapon himself. Then he fired.

Again a cheer arose aboard the Brigadier. Frank's shot had been successful. The shell struck the submersible squarely amidships, and carried away the periscope.

"Fire!" cried Frank, and the other guns broke into action.

Again there was a wild cheer.

The submarine began to settle a few moments later. Men emerged from below and sprang into the sea.

"Lower a boat!" cried Jack. "I want a few of those fellows."

A boat was lowered instantly and strong hands pulled it toward the Germans floundering in the water.

By this time the lifeboats that had escaped the German fire came alongside the Brigadier and the occupants climbed aboard the destroyer. These were quickly fitted out with dry clothing. It developed that there had been three women passengers aboard the Hazelton and all of these had been saved. A dozen members of the crew, however, had been killed by the enemy in the lifeboats.

Jack assigned quarters to the victims as quickly as he was able, and then calling his officers about him, awaited the return of the boat which had gone after the Germans who had leaped into the sea.

"If the act I have just seen is a sample of the German heart," Jack said, "I never want another German within sight of me so long as I live."

## CHAPTER VI

## CHANGED ORDERS

As the Germans came aboard—ten of them—they were herded before Jack. They stood there sullenly, their eyes on the deck. One of them wore a heavily braided and imposing uniform. Jack addressed him.

"You are the commander of that submarine?" he questioned.

"I was," answered the German.

"You were, what?" asked Jack sharply.

"I was the commander."

"You don't seem to catch my meaning," said Jack, taking a step forward. "When you speak to me say 'sir.'"

"Then you shall say 'sir' to me," said the German.

"Oh, no I won't," Jack declared. "I never say sir to a murderer."

The German's eyes lighted angrily.

"It would be well to be more careful of your words," he said.

"Nevertheless," said Jack, "I repeat them. You, are a murderer, and as such should be hanged at once. I'm not sure it is in my province to string you up, but I'm strongly tempted to do so and take the consequences."

"But I guess you won't," sneered the German.

"Then don't try me too far," said Jack quietly. "To my mind, men like you and your cowardly followers should be put out of the way the same as a mad dog; and certainly there is no law against killing a dog."

"I warn you," said the German, taking a step nearer the lad, "to be more choice in your words."

"Silence!" Jack thundered, "and don't you dare step toward me unless I tell you to do so." He turned to Frank. "Take those men below and put them in irons," he ordered.

Frank stepped forward to obey, and again the German commander protested.

"You can't do that," he said. "My men are prisoners of war and as such are entitled to all the usual courtesies."

"They are, eh?" asked Jack. "Then I'll modify that order a bit, temporarily, Mr. Chadwick, will you kindly bring irons for this man here," and he indicated the German officer. "I want his men and all our passengers to see how he looks in shackles, which he should have been made to wear long ago."

Frank hurried away. The German commander, after taking one step back at Jack's words, stepped quickly forward again. His hand went to his side and he produced a long knife. Then he sprang.

Jack smiled slightly, stepped quickly to one side and with his left hand caught the German's knife arm. He twisted sharply, and the knife dropped to the deck.

Jack released his hold and the German staggered back. Deliberately Jack cuffed the man across the face with his right hand, then with his left. Twice more he did this, following the German as he retreated across the deck.

"Let that teach you," he said, "that attempting to stab a British naval officer is very bad business. But here comes something that will teach you more," and he pointed to Frank, who reappeared at that moment followed by two sailors bearing heavy chains. "These irons," Jack continued, "will show you just what is in store for you when you are landed in England. Hold out your hands."

The German did so. Quickly handcuffs were snapped on.

"Shackle his legs," said Jack.

The sailors needed no urging. Quickly the German's legs were shackled with the heavy iron. Jack took a couple of steps back and surveyed his prisoner.

"If you had been dressed up in those several years ago," he said, "I've no doubt lots of innocent women and children now at the bottom of the sea would be alive still."

The German commander scowled, but he said nothing.

"Now, Frank," said Jack, "you will take the other prisoners below and put them in irons. I guess our friend here will no longer object."

The German sailors were led below, where they were soon safely chained and Frank returned to the bridge.

"Kindly pass the word for all the passengers and the crew to come on deck, Mr. Hetherton," ordered Jack.

The second officer obeyed and soon the deck was crowded. The German commander became the center of an angry group.

"I've just called you all here," said Jack, "that you may cast your eyes upon one of the kaiser's paid murderers. It is men like this who have made an outcast of Germany. Not satisfied with killing in battle, they fire on helpless lifeboats, sending women and children as well as unarmed noncombatants to the bottom of the sea. In fact, it is men like this, or a man like this, who so recently took a heavy toll in lives from the crew of the Hazelton, after the vessel had been put out of commission."

There was an angry murmur among the crowd on deck.

"Hang him," said a voice.

The German officer's face turned a chalky white.

"I'd be pleased to do so," said Jack, "were it not for the fact that I must retain him as a prisoner of war and turn him over to the proper authorities. However, it wouldn't surprise me a bit if he were tried for murder and hanged, and I'm not sure that even such a fate isn't too good for him."

"Hang him!" came a voice from the crowd again.

"No," said Jack quietly, "it can't be done. Take him away."

These last words were addressed to Lieutenant Hetherton, who stepped forward and took the German commander by the arm.

"Come on," he said somewhat roughly.

The German commander was led below, where he was made secure.

The passengers and crew rescued from the Hazelton dispersed and Jack held a consultation with his officers.

"If we were not so far from land," he said, "I would land those we have rescued. As it stands, I am under rush orders, so I am afraid I shall have to take them to America."

"That cannot be helped, sir," said Lieutenant Hetherton. "I am sure they will understand that, sir."

"I think so, too," agreed Frank.

"At all events," said Jack, "there seems nothing else to do under the circumstances. Ring for full speed ahead, Mr. Chadwick."

Frank did so.

At that moment the radio operator again emerged from below and hurried to Jack.

"Admiralty orders, sir," he said, passing a slip of paper to the commander of the Brigadier.

Jack read the paper quickly, then turned to Frank with a sharp command.

"Slow to half speed," he said. "Then come about and head for Dover."

Frank asked no questions. He knew that Jack would explain the reason for the change soon enough. Besides, the matter was none of his business. He gave the necessary orders. Jack turned to the second officer.

"Will you take the bridge, Mr. Hetherton? Mr. Chadwick, please come to my cabin."

The lads went below together.

"Now," said Frank, after he had taken a seat, "what's it all about?"

"Well," was Jack's reply, "the admiralty wants the Brigadier back in Dover. That's all I know about it. I'm instructed to report to Lord Hastings immediately on my return."

"No other explanation?"

"No."

"Funny," commented Frank. "Must be something up, though."

"So it would seem. However, I guess we'll learn soon enough. Hope they are not going to deprive me of my command."

"No fear, I guess," declared Frank.

The return trip was made in record time and without incident. Jack saw the victims of the Hazelton landed safely and then, turning the ship over to Lieutenant Hetherton, went ashore with Frank to report to Lord Hastings.

The latter greeted them with a wry smile.

"It seems that my warning to America is not to be delivered after all," he said.

"And why, sir?" asked Jack. "Are you not still convinced that the warning is necessary?"

"I am," declared Lord Hastings, "but, as I told you, I was sending the warning without knowledge of the Admiralty. Naturally, then, when it was announced that the Brigadier was to be recalled to take part in other operations, I could not announce that you carried secret dispatches from me."

"I see," said Jack. "And what is the nature of the other operation?"

"It is a desperate undertaking," said Lord Hastings slowly, "and one that, at first, I was tempted to advise against. And still, if successful it will do much toward insuring an allied victory."

"Since when have you become so cautious, sir?" asked Frank with a smile.

"It's not a matter of caution, Frank," replied Lord Hastings. "It's simply a matter of prudence. In a word, the Admiralty is determined to block the harbors of Ostend and Zeebrugge."

Frank was on his feet and clapping his hands.

"Fine!" he exclaimed. "I don't see why it hasn't been done sooner. I remember what Hobson did to the Spanish fleet at Santiago in the Spanish-American war."

"It's an exploit of the same nature," Lord Hastings admitted, "though it will be attended with even greater danger. If successful, as I say, it will do inestimable good. The admiralty has been training specially for this move for months, but the matter has now come to a head."

"And how does it happen that we shall be fortunate enough to lend a hand?" asked Jack.

"My fault, I suppose," returned Lord Hastings. "Admiral Keyes, the day after your departure, was bemoaning the fact that one ship had been taken away from him at the last moment. I said that if Captain Templeton and the Brigadier were here, you could easily replace the other vessel. The admiral was of the opinion that you had not had the necessary training. I said you didn't need it. Apparently he was convinced, for the next I heard you had been recalled to Dover. Thus, through talking too much, I balked my own plans."

"Perhaps," said Frank, "it won't be too late for the other when the harbors of Ostend and Zeebrugge have been sealed."

"But perhaps you won't come back," said Lord Hastings.

"Oh, we'll be back, never fear," grinned Jack. "But what are we to do now?"

"You will report to Admiral Keyes aboard the Warwick at once. If you return safely, report to me. Good-bye and good luck."

The lads shook hands with Lord Hastings and left him.

"Here," said Frank, "is what I call a piece of luck."

CHAPTER VII

A BIT OF EXPLANATION

It is probable that the sealing of the harbors of Ostend and Zeebrugge, two of the most important German submarine bases, was one of the greatest feats of the whole European war. The attempt was extremely hazardous and could never have been successful except for the gallantry and heroism of the British crews.

Not the least of the bravest among them were Jack and Frank and the other officers and crew of the destroyer Brigadier. It is true that the operation has been planned primarily with the idea of having the destroyer Daffodil in line, but it was the withdrawal of this vessel that permitted Jack and Frank to have a hand in the operation.

In order that all parts of the naval service might share in the expedition, representative bodies of men had been drawn from the Grand Fleet, the three home depots, the Royal marine artillery and light infantry. The ships and torpedo craft were furnished by the Dover patrol, which was reinforced by vessels from the Harwich force and the French and American navies. The Royal Australian navy and the admiralty experimental station at Stratford and Dover were also represented.

A force thus composed and armed, obviously needed collective training and special preparation to adapt both the men and their weapons to their purpose. With these objects, the blocking ships and the storming forces were assembled toward the end of February, and from the fourth of April on in the West Swim Anchorage—where training especially adapted to the plan of operation was given—and the organization of the expedition was carried on.

The material as it was prepared was used to make the training practical and was itself tested thereby. Moreover, valuable practice was afforded by endeavors to carry out the project on two previous occasions, on which the conditions of wind and weather compelled its postponement, and much was learned from these temporary failures.

The Hindustan, at first at Chatham and later at the Swim, was the parent ship and training depot. After the second attempt, when it became apparent that there would be a long delay, the Dominion joined the Hindustan and the pressure upon the available accommodation was relieved by the transfer of about 350 seamen and marines to her.

Two special craft, Liverpool ferry steamers, Iris and Gloucester, were selected after a long search by Captain Herbert Grant. They were selected because of their shallow draft, with a view in the first place to their pushing the Vindictive, which was to bear the brunt of the work, alongside Zeebrugge Mole; to the possibility, should the Vindictive be sunk, of their bringing away all her crew and the landing parties; and to their ability to maneuver in shallow water or clear of mine fields or torpedoes. The blocking ships and the Vindictive were especially prepared for their work long before the start.

Vice-Admiral Sir Roger Keyes devoted personal attention and time to working out the plan of operations and the preparation of the personnel and material. Rear Admiral Cecil F. Dampier, second in command of the Dover flotilla, and Commodore Algernon Boyle, chief of staff, gave considerable assistance.

When, as vice-admiral of the Dover patrol, Admiral Keyes first began to prepare for the operation, it became apparent that without an effective system of smoke screening such an attack could hardly hope to succeed. The system of making smoke previously employed in the Dover patrol was unsuitable for a night operation, as this production generated a fierce flame, and no other means of making an effective smoke screen was available. Nevertheless Wing Commander Brock, at last devised the way.

The commander-in-chief of the Grand Fleet, Admiral Beatty, sent to Admiral Keyes a picked body of officers and men. Support also was received from the neighboring commands at Portsmouth and the Nore, the adjutant general, Royal Marines, and the depot at Chatham. The rear-admiral commanding the Harwich force sent a flotilla leader and six destroyers, besides protecting the northern flank of the area in which operations were to be conducted.

To afford protection at a certain point in the route and to maintain the aids to navigation during the approach and retirement of the expedition, a force consisting of the flotilla leaders Scott and the destroyers Ulleswater, Teazer and Stork, and the light cruiser Attentive, flying the pennant of Commodore Boyle, was organized. This force, as it developed, was instrumental in patroling and directing the movements of detached craft in both directions, and relieved Admiral Keyes of all anxiety on that score.

At the moment of departing the forces were disposed as follows:

In the Swim—For the attack on the Zeebrugge Mole: Vindictive, Iris, Gloucester. To block the Bruges canal: Thetis, Interprid and Iphigenia. To block the entrance to Ostend: Sirius and Brilliant.

At Dover—Warwick, flagship of Vice-Admiral Keyes; Phoebe, North Star, Brigadier, Trident, Mansfield, Whirlwind, Myngs, Velox, Morris, Moorsom, Melpomene, Tempest and Tetrarch.

To damage Zeebrugge—Submarines C-1 and C-3.

A special picket boat to rescue crews of C-1 and C-3.

Minesweeper Lingfield to take off surplus steaming parties of block ships, which had 100 miles to steam.

Eighteen coastal motorboats.

Thirty-three motor launches.

To bombard vicinity of Zeebrugge—Monitors Erebus and Terror.

To attend monitors—Termagant, Truculent, and Manly.

Outer patrol off Zeebrugge—Attentive, Scot, Ulleswater, Teazer and Stork.

At Dunkirk—Monitors for bombarding Ostend: Marshal Soult, Lord Clive, Prince Eugene, General Sraufurd, M-24 and M-26.

For operating off Ostend—Swift, Faulknor, Matchless, Mastiff and Afridi.

The British destroyers Mentor, Lightfoot, Zubian and French torpedo boats Lestin, Capitaine Mehl, Francis Garnier, Roux and Boucier to accompany the monitors.

There were in addition to these, three American destroyers—the Taylor, the Alert and the Cyprus.

Eighteen British motor launches for smoke screening duty inshore and rescue work, and six for attending big monitors.

Four French motor launches attending M-24 and M-26 and five coastal motor boats.

Navigational aids having been established on the routes, the forces from the Swim and Dover were directed to join Admiral Keyes off the Goodwin Sands and to proceed in company to a rendezvous, and thereafter as requisite to their respective stations.

Those from Dunkirk were given their orders by the commodore.

An operation time table was issued to govern the movements of all the forces. Wireless signals were prohibited, visual signals of every sort were reduced to a minimum and maneuvering prearranged as far as foresight could provide.

With few and slight delays the program for the passage was carried out as laid down, the special aids to navigation being found of great assistance.

The Harwich force, under Rear-Admiral Tyrwhitt, was posted to cover the operations and prevent interference from the north.

Jack and Frank, having reported to Admiral Keyes upon leaving Lord Hastings, had received necessary instructions as to their part in the raid. They had passed the word to the other officers of the Brigadier, who in turn had informed members of the crew what was about to happen.

There was wild cheering among the British tars on the Brigadier when they learned they were to have a hand in one of the greatest and most dangerous enterprises attempted in the whole war. Needless to say, Jack and Frank also were immensely pleased.

"Tell you what, Jack," said Frank, after they had returned aboard the Brigadier, "it seems to me as though your work had come to the ears of the Admiralty with a vengeance."

"Oh, I guess that isn't it," Jack laughed. "They just happened to need another ship and picked on me. That's all."

"Perhaps," Frank admitted. "But just the same it seems that we are always in the midst of things. I wouldn't call it all luck, if I were you."

"Well, it's not good judgment, that much is certain," said Jack. "For good judgment would tell me to keep in a safe place as long as possible."

"If you want to know what I think about it," said Frank, "this raid is going to be one of the greatest blows struck at the enemy."

"It certainly will do the enemy a lot of harm if it's successful," Jack confessed.

"It'll be successful all right. I can feel that."

"A hunch, eh?" laughed Jack.

"Call it what you like. Nevertheless, I am absolutely certain Admiral Keyes will not fail. And what are the Germans going to do for submarine bases if Ostend and Zeebrugge are bottled up?"

"Maybe we'll catch most of them in there," said Jack hopefully.

"They won't be able to get out again if we do," declared Frank.

"Right," Jack agreed, "and the ones that are outside won't be able to get back in again."

"So you see," Frank continued, "we have them coming and going, as we say in America."

"I see," said Jack.

"And what time are we to start?" asked Frank. "You must remember you were in private conference with Admiral Keyes. You're a captain now, and the big fellows talk to you. I'm still only a lieutenant."

"The passage will most likely be made by daylight," said Jack. "That has been decided in order that we may do our work there under the cover of darkness so far as possible. Of course, this may be changed, but that's the way the plan lies now."

"Strikes me we are taking a pretty big force along, from what you say."

"Necessary, I guess," said Jack. "It seems that the admiral has overlooked nothing that will go toward making the attack a success."

"Well, we can't start any too soon to suit me," declared Frank. "When do you expect to get orders to move?"

"I'm not certain, but I wouldn't be surprised to receive them early in the morning."

As it developed Jack was a good prophet.

Bright and early next morning, a small boat approached the Brigadier. A few moments later an officer came aboard and presented Jack with a document. Then he departed.

Jack read the paper, then leaped to the bridge.

"To your post, Mr. Chadwick," he called to Frank, who had been standing near by. "Pipe all men to quarters and signal for half speed ahead."

The passage was about to begin.

## CHAPTER VIII

## THE ATTACK BEGINS

The main force was divided into three columns. The center column was led by the Vindictive, with the Brigadier second and the Iris in tow, followed by the five blocking ships and the paddle mine-sweeper Lingfield, escorting five motor launches for taking off the surplus steaming parties of the blocking ships. The starboard column was led by the Warwick, flying the flag of Admiral Keyes, followed by the Phoebe and North Star, which three ships were to cover the Vindictive from torpedo attack while the storming operations were in progress.

The submarines were towed by the Trident and Mansfield. The Tempest escorted the two Ostend block ships.

The port column was led by the Whirlwind, followed by Myngs and Moorsom, which ships were to patrol to the northward of Zeebrugge; and the Tetrarch, also to escort the Ostend block ships. Every craft was towing one or more coastal motor boats, and between the columns were motor launches.

The greater part of the passage, as Jack had explained, had to be carried out in broad daylight, with the consequent likelihood of discovery by enemy aircraft or submarines. This risk was largely countered by the escort of all the scouting escort under Admiral Keyes' command.

On arrival at a certain position, it being then apparent that the conditions were favorable and that there was every prospect of carrying through the enterprise on schedule, a short prearranged wireless signal was made to the detached forces that the program would be adhered to.

On arrival at a position a mile and a half short of where Commodore Boyle's force was stationed, the whole force stopped for fifteen minutes to enable the surplus steaming parties of the block ships to be disembarked and the coastal motor boats slipped. These and the motor launches then proceeded in execution of previous orders. On resuming the course, the Warwick and Whirlwind, followed by the destroyers, drew ahead on either bow to clear the passage of enemy outpost vessels.

When the Vindictive arrived at a position where it was necessary to alter her course for the Mole, the Warwick, Phoebe and North Star swung to starboard and cruised in the vicinity of the Mole until after the final withdrawal of all the attacking forces. During the movement and through the subsequent operations, the Warwick was maneuvered to place smoke screens wherever they seemed to be most required, and when the wind shifted from northeast to southwest, her services in this respect were particularly valuable.

The monitors Erebus and Terror, with the destroyers Termagant, Truculent and Manly, were stationed at a position suitable for the long range bombardment of Zeebrugge in co-operation with the attack.

Similarly, the monitors Marshal Soult, General Sraufurd, Prince Eugene and Lord Clive, and the small monitors M-21, M-24 and M-26 were stationed in suitable positions to bombard specified batteries. These craft were attended by the British destroyers Mentor, Lightfoot and Zubian, and the French Capitaine Mehl, Francis Garnier, Roux and Bouclier. The bombardment that ensued was undoubtedly useful in keeping down the fire of the shore batteries.

The attack on the Mole was primarily intended to distract the enemy's attention from the ships engaged in blocking the Bruges canal. Its immediate objectives were, first, the capture of the four 1-inch batteries at the sea end of the Mole, which bore a serious menace to the passage of the block ships, and, second, the doing of as much damage to the material on the Mole as time would permit, for it was not the intention of Admiral Keyes to remain on the Mole after the primary object of the expedition had been accomplished.

The attack was to consist of two parts: The landing of storming and demolition parties and the destruction of the iron viaduct between the shore and the stone Mole.

The units detailed for the attack were:

H.M.S. Vindictive, Captain Alfred F.B. Carpenter; the Brigadier, Captain Jack Templeton; special steamers Iris, Commander Valentine Gibbs; Gloucester, Lieutenant H.G. Campbell, the latter detailed to push the Vindictive alongside the Mole and keep her there as long as might be necessary.

Submarines C-3 and C-1, commanded by Lieutenants Richard Sanford and Aubrey Newbold, respectively, attended by picket boat under Lieutenant Commander Francis H. Sanford.

Besides these, a flotilla of twenty-four motor launches and eight coastal motorboats were told off for rescue work and to make smoke screens or lay smoke floats, and nine more coastal motorboats to attack the Mole and enemy vessels inside it.

At 11.40 p.m. on April 22, 1918, the coastal motorboats detailed to lay the first smoke screen ran in to very close range and proceeded to lay smoke floats and by other methods make the necessary "fog." These craft immediately were under fire, and only their small size and great speed saved them from destruction.

At this moment the Blankenberghe light buoy was abeam of the Vindictive and the enemy had presumably seen or heard the approaching forces. Star shells lighted the heavens. But still no enemy patrol craft were sighted. At this time the wind had been from the northeast, and therefore favorable to the success of the smoke screens. It now died away and began to blow from a southerly direction.

Many of the smoke floats laid just off the Mole extension were sunk by the fire of the enemy, which now began to grow in volume. This, in conjunction with the wind, lessened the effectiveness of the smoke screen.

At 11.56 the Vindictive, the Brigadier close behind, having just passed through a smoke screen, sighted the Mole in the semi-darkness about three hundred yards off on the port bow. Speed was increased to full and the course of both vessels altered so that, allowing for cross tide, the Vindictive would make good a closing course of forty-five degrees to the Mole. The Vindictive purposely withheld her fire to avoid being discovered, but almost at the moment of her emerging from the smoke the enemy opened fire.

So promptly, under the orders of the commander, was this replied to by the port 6-inch battery, the upper deck pompoms and the gun in the foretop that the firing on both sides appeared to be almost simultaneous.

The Brigadier, under Jack's command, opened fire at almost the same moment. Heavy shells flew screaming into the enemy lines. German projectiles began to kick up the water close to the Vindictive and the Brigadier. But in the first few volleys, none of the enemy shells found their marks. Jack was conning the ship from the port forward, the flame-thrower hut. Frank, with directions as to handling of the ship should Jack be disabled, was in the conning tower, from which the Brigadier was being steered.

At one minute after midnight on April 23, the program time for attack being midnight, the Vindictive was put alongside the Mole and the starboard anchor was let go.

At this time the noise of cannonading was terrific. During the previous few minutes, the ship had been hit by a large number of shells, which had resulted in heavy casualties.

As there was some doubt as to the starboard anchor having gone clear, the port anchor was dropped close to the foot of the Mole and the cable bowsed-to, with less than a shackle out. A three-knot tide was running past the Mole, and the scene alongside, created by the slight swell, caused the ship to roll. There was an interval of three or four minutes before the Brigadier or the Gloucester could arrive and commence to push the Vindictive bodily alongside.

During the interval the Vindictive could not be got close enough for the special Mole anchors to hook and it was a very trying period. Many of the brows had been broken by shell fire and the heavy roll had broken the foremost Mole anchor as it was being placed. The two foremost brows, however, reached the wall and enabled storming parties, led by Lieutenant-Commander Bryan F. Adams, to land and run out alongside them, closely followed by the Royal marines.

It was at this juncture that a slight change was made in the original program. It developed, as the first storming party moved out, that Commander Adams' men were not in sufficient strength for the work ahead. Captain Carpenter of the Vindictive called for support from the Brigadier. Jack acted promptly.

"Lieutenant Chadwick!" he called.

Frank stepped forward and saluted.

"You will take one hundred men and join the storming party," said Jack.

At this moment the Brigadier was rubbing close to the Vindictive. This was fortunate at the moment, for there was then no other means by which a party from the Brigadier could reach the Mole.

Hurriedly Frank gathered the men, and then leaped from his own vessel to the deck of the Vindictive. A moment later they joined Commander Adams and his party.

Owing to the rolling of the ship, a most disconcerting motion was imparted to the brows, the outer ends of which were "sawing" considerably on the Mole parapet. Officers and men were equipped with Lewis guns, bombs, ammunition, etc., and were under heavy machine-gun fire at close range; add to this a drop of thirty feet between the ship and the Mole, and some idea of the conditions which had to be faced may be realized.

Yet the storming of the Mole was carried out without the slightest delay and without any apparent consideration of self preservation. Some of the first men on the Mole dropped in their tracks under the German fire, but the others pushed on, with the object of hauling one of the large Mole anchors across the parapet.

The Brigadier arrived alongside the Mole three minutes after Frank and his men had leaped to the deck of the other ship, followed by the little Iris. Both suffered less in their approach, the Vindictive occupying all the enemy's attention. The Gloucester also came up now to push the Vindictive bodily on to the Mole to enable her to be secured, after doing which the Gloucester landed her parties over that ship. Her men disembarked from her bows on to the Vindictive, as it was found essential to continue to push the Vindictive on to the Mole throughout the entire action.

This duty was magnificently carried out. Without the assistance of the Gloucester very few of the storming parties from the Vindictive could have landed, or could have re-embarked.

The landing from the Iris was made under even more trying circumstances. She rolled heavily in the sea, which rendered the use of the scaling ladders very difficult. But at this time, according to calculations, enough men had been landed to complete the work.

The fighting on the Mole became hand-to-hand.

## CHAPTER IX

## THE BATTLE CONTINUES

A shell suddenly exploded among the Vindictive's foremost 7.5-inch howitzer's marine crew. Many were killed or wounded. A naval crew from a 6-inch gun took their places and were almost annihilated.

At this time the Vindictive was being hit every few seconds, chiefly in the upper works, from which the splinters caused many casualties. It was difficult for the British to locate the guns which were doing the most damage, but Jack, from the Brigadier, with men posted in the fortop of the vessel, kept up a continuous fire with pompoms and Lewis machine-guns, changing rapidly from one target to another in an attempt to destroy the guns that were raking the Vindictive fore and aft.

Two heavy shells struck the foretop of the Brigadier almost simultaneously. Half a dozen men were killed. A score of others were wounded.

To return for a moment to Frank and his men.

The attack on the Mole had been designed to be carried out by a storming force to prepare the way for, and afterward to cover and protect, the operations of a second force, which was to carry out the actual work of destruction. The storming force, which had embarked in the Vindictive, was now reinforced by a hundred British tars from the Brigadier, headed by Frank, and additional sailors from the Iris and Gloucester.

For the first time it was now ascertained that the Vindictive, in anchoring off the Mole, had over-run her station and was berthed some four hundred yards farther to the westward than had been intended.

It had been realized beforehand that the Vindictive might not exactly reach the exact position mapped out, but the fact that the landing was carried out in an unexpected place, combined with the heavy losses already sustained by the vessel, seriously disorganized the attacking force. The intention had been to land the storming parties right on top of the 4 1-inch guns in position on the seaward end of the Mole, the silencing of which was of the first importance, as they menaced the approach of the block ships.

The leading block ship had been timed to pass the lighthouse twenty-five minutes after the Vindictive came alongside. This period of time proved insufficient to organize and carry through an attack against the enemy on the seaward end of the Mole, the enemy, it developed, being able to bring heavy machine-gun fire to bear on the attacking forces. As a result the block ships, when they approached, came under an unexpected fire from the light guns on the Mole extension, though the 4.1-inch batteries on the Mole had remained silent.

Commander Adams, followed by Frank and his men, were the first to land. At that moment no enemy was seen on the Mole. They found themselves on a pathway on the Mole parapet about eight feet wide, with a wall four feet high on the seaward side, and an iron railing on the Mole side. From this pathway, there was a drop of fifteen feet on the Mole proper.

Followed by his men and Frank and the latter's command, Commander Adams went alongside the parapet to the left, where he found a lookout station or control, with a range finder behind and above it.

"Blow it up!" he shouted to Frank, who was close to him at that moment.

Frank gave a command to one of his men. A moment later there was an explosion and the station disappeared as though by magic.

Near the lookout station aft iron ladder led down to the Mole and three of Frank's men descended it. Frank went with them. Below they encountered half a dozen of the enemy.

It was no time to hesitate and Frank knew it.

"Bombs, men," he said simply.

Three hands drew back, then were brought forward. Three hand grenades dropped among the foes. There were three short blasts, and when the smoke cleared away, there were no Germans to be seen at that point. Then Frank and his men rejoined the others.

The situation now was that Commander Adams, Frank, their few men and a few Lewis guns, were beyond the lookout station protected from machine-gun fire from the direction of the Mole head, but exposed to fire from their own destroyers, alongside the Mole.

Commander Adams called Frank to him.

"We're in a ticklish position here, lieutenant," he said. "We're in danger of being shot down by our own guns. At the same time, if we move from behind this station, we are not in sufficient strength to drive the enemy away."

"Why not risk our own, fire, sir," said Frank, "and ask for reinforcements."

"That's a request that will have to be made in person," said Commander Adams, "and it will be rather risky."

"I'll be glad to try it sir," said Frank.

Commander Adams shrugged.

"It'd about as broad as it is long," he said. "If you're shot on the way I guess it will be no worse than dying here. Go ahead, if you wish."

Now to gain the needed reinforcements, Frank knew that it would be necessary to return to the side of the Vindictive. To reach that vessel it would be necessary to pass through places exposed to enemy machine-gun fire. However, at the moment, the German guns covering those particular spots were silent, so Frank decided to take the risk.

He set out at a run. At first his appearance was apparently unnoticed, but soon a rain of bullets poured after him. Two or three times the lad threw himself to the ground just in time. He was on his feet again a moment later, however, and at last reached his destination safely.

As the lad reached the side of the Vindictive he saw a second storming party coming over the side, equipped with Lewis machine-guns and rifles and hand bombs. Frank approached the commander of the party, Lieutenant-Commander Hastings, and outlined the plight of those he had left behind.

"Come with us," said Commander Hastings, "we'll soon clear those fellows out back there."

Machine-guns were wheeled into position and the British raked the German line wherever heads appeared. In this method they relieved the hard-pressed party under Commander Adams.

The first objective of the storming party ashore was a fortified zone situated about a hundred and fifty yards from the seaward end of the Mole proper. Its capture was of the first importance, as an enemy holding it could bring a heavy fire to bear on the parties still to land from the Vindictive.

Commander Adams ordered an advance.

Frank was placed in command of the left wing of the little army, Commander Hastings of the right wing. Commander Adams led the center himself. The British spread out.

"Charge!" cried Commander Adams.

"Charge!" repeated Frank and Commander Hastings a moment later.

The British seamen went forward on the double, bayonets fixed.

From out of their fortified positions the Germans sprang forth to meet them, machine-guns from behind covering their advance. At the same moment Frank ordered his own machine-guns wheeled into position, and swept the advancing enemy with a hail of bullets.

But neither side paid much attention to this rain of lead, and directly the fighting became too close for either side to utilize its machine-guns. Steel clashed on steel. Revolvers in the hands of the officers cracked. Men fell to the right and to the left.

For a moment it appeared that the attacking force must be hurled back by the very weight of the numbers against them. But they rallied after one brief moment in which it seemed that they must yield, and hurled themselves forward again. This time there was no stopping them.

Directly the thin German line wavered. Then it broke, and the enemy dashed for the protection of their fortified position at top speed. But the British sailors kept close on their heels, and they reached the coveted spot at almost the same time. There the fighting was resumed, but after a short resistance the enemy again retreated, leaving the position in the hands of the British.

Immediately Commander Adams ordered the machine-guns which had been abandoned by the foe in his flight turned on them and the Germans were mowed down in great numbers.

Having gained his objective, Commander Adams ordered his men to proceed down the Mole and hold a position there so as to cover the operations of the party of destruction, which was now hard at work. To expel these British, German troops were now advancing from the landward end of the Mole.

The destruction of the viaduct by the submarine C-3 had been designed to aid the efforts of the landing party by preventing reinforcements reaching the Mole from the shore. Owing to the Vindictive coming alongside to landward of this zone, Commander Adams' men were now faced with a double duty of preventing an enemy attack from the shore and of themselves attacking a second fortified zone ahead of them. The casualties already sustained were so great that the Iris could not remain alongside the Vindictive to land her company of Royal Marines. This left insufficient men in the early stages of the landing to carry out both operations.

The situation was a difficult one, for to attack the fortified zone first might enable the enemy to advance up the Mole and seize positions abreast of the Vindictive, with the most serious consequences to the whole landing force, whereas, by not attacking the fortified positions, the guns at the Mole head could not be prevented from firing at the block ships.

Therefore, Commander Adams instructed Frank to secure the landward side, at the same time instructing Commander Hastings to attack the fortified zone. Commander Adams knew that he was taking a long chance by thus dividing his forces, but in no other manner, it seemed to him, could the success of the expedition be assured.

Frank led his men forward promptly. Apparently the Germans had not realized the full strength of the British attack on the Mole, for no effort had been made to get reinforcements to the men there from shore. Consequently, Frank's work was not so hard as that set for Commander Hastings.

The few Germans who were guarding the landward side of the Mole fired one volley at Frank's party, then turned and took to their heels.

"By George! Pretty soft!" said Frank.

He led his men to the positions recently vacated by the enemy, and then sat down to await further instructions from Commander Adams.

Commander Hastings, on the other hand, had hard work in taking the fortified positions from the foe. Nevertheless he succeeded, due to the heroic efforts of his men. Commander Adams surveyed the field carefully.

"Well," he told himself, "I guess we've done the best we can. We'll stick here till we get the signal to withdraw."

## CHAPTER X

## THE RAID SUCCESSFUL

The platoon which was commanded by Commander Adams was officially designated as No. 1; that commanded by Frank as No. 2 and that commanded by Commander Hastings as No. 3.

Units were now landing rapidly and No. 7 platoon succeeded in placing heavy scaling ladders in positions, and then formed up to support Nos. 9 and 10 platoons. Numbers 11 and 12 platoons were dispatched along the parapet, and reached the lookout station, where they were checked. Commander Adams and his men, who had again united with the parties commanded by Frank and Commander Hastings, were some forty to fifty yards ahead of them, and both parties could make no headway along the exposed parapet. Meanwhile No. 5 platoon, which had been recalled from its advanced position, with Nos. 7 and 8 platoons were forming up on the Mole for an assault on the fortified zone and the 4.1-inch battery at the Mole head. This attack was launched, but before it could be developed the general recall was sounded.

There was a cheer from the men. They knew by the sounding of the recall at this moment meant that the expedition had been a success. Otherwise the fighting on the Mole would have continued.

The units fell back in good order, taking their wounded with them. The passing of the men from the Mole on to the parapet by means of the scaling ladders was rendered hazardous by the enemy opening fire at that portion of the Mole. Several ladders were destroyed.

The men were sent across in small batches from the comparative shelter afforded by long distance fire from the battleships. Such rushes were made as far as possible in the intervals between the bursts of German fire.

The landing parties re-embarked in the manner which they had left their ships—climbing to the deck of the Vindictive and then proceeding to their deck of the Vindictive and then proceeding to their various ships by small boats.

This undertaking was hazardous, too, for enemy shells were falling all about. Nevertheless, the most of the men reached their ship in safety, and from the flagship came the signal to retreat.

Upon returning to the Brigadier, Frank surveyed his own men. There had been few casualties among them. Less than a dozen men had been killed and left behind. Of wounded Frank counted fifteen. Immediately he ascended to the bridge to report to Jack.

Jack greeted his chum with a smile. Although the Brigadier had been in the midst of the battle, and many German shells had found their marks aboard her, Jack was as cool and unruffled as before the battle started.

"What luck, Frank?" he asked.

"Good," Frank replied. "We held the Mole until ordered back. And you?"

"The best of luck. I've stuck tight to the Vindictive through the heat of the battle, and I believe our guns have done some damage."

"And the block ships?" asked Frank.

"They have been sunk at the mouths of both harbors, I am informed. The raid has been a complete success."

At that moment came the recall signal from the flagship.

"See," said Jack, "there's proof of it. If we had not been successful, the recall would not have been sounded yet. There is still plenty of time if we needed it, and our damage has not been great enough to leave the job unfinished."

Jack was right. The harbors of Ostend and Zeebrugge had been effectually sealed. No longer would enemy U-Boats make nightly raids into the North Sea, only to scurry back to their bases when it grew light. As a submarine base, Zeebrugge was extinct. So, for that matter, was Ostend.

That the success of the British expedition had been a severe blow to the Germans goes without saying. No other single feat since the beginning of the war had done so much to dishearten them; and there is little doubt that the sealing of their submarine bases did much toward hastening the end of the war.

British losses in the raid had been severe. The Vindictive, which had led the attack, had literally been shot to pieces and it was a miracle how she remained afloat. The Brigadier, also, had suffered severely, but her condition was not so bad that a few months in drydock would not be sufficient to make her whole again.

A dozen or more of the little motorboats and coastal patrol vessels had been sunk, and the loss of life had been heavy. Several others of the destroyers had been badly damaged, but there was not one of the larger vessels sunk or crippled so badly that she could not return to her home port.

It still lacked an hour of daylight when the allied fleet drew off, its work accomplished; and behind in the ports now sealed, the anger of the Germans flared forth anew.

The damaged British ships were immediately put into drydock in British ports, and Jack and Frank at once returned to Dover to report to Lord Hastings. The latter greeted the lads with outstretched hands.

"It was a gallant exploit," he exclaimed, "and I am sure both you boys had important roles to play."

"I guess we did, sir," Frank admitted. "At the same time, I'm glad to be safely back here again."

"I suppose, sir," said Jack, "now that the enemy submarines caught outside are without bases, there is little fear of their attempting the trans-Atlantic trip?"

"On the contrary," said Lord Hastings, "they are more likely than ever to do so."

"But they must have a base, sir," protested Frank.

"Not necessarily," smiled Lord Hastings.

"Then how will they replenish their supplies of food and fuel?"

"Well," said Lord Hastings, "if they can snare a victim every three or four days it should be enough. From a merchant ship they can get all the food and fuel they need before sinking her."

"That's so, by George!" Frank exclaimed.

"It stands to reason," said Lord Hastings, "that those submarines which were not bottled up in the harbors have been warned not to return. Now, it wouldn't surprise me a bit if they headed directly for America."

Jack grew thoughtful.

"It's too bad," he said at last, "that the Brigadier was so crippled that we cannot resume our interrupted voyage."

Lord Hastings smiled.

"I understand she is in pretty bad shape," he said. "So you don't think you can go now, eh?"

"I'm afraid not, sir. A fellow can't cross the ocean except in a ship."

"True enough. But why are you in Dover now?"

"Why, sir?" Jack exclaimed. "Because we were instructed to report to you."

"Exactly," said Lord Hastings; "and in your pocket, I presume, you have the same packet of papers the admiralty wishes turned over to Secretary Daniels of the American navy department?"

Jack clapped a hand to his coat pocket.

"By George! I had forgotten all about them," he said.

"So I imagined. But it is my guess that the navy department still wishes those papers delivered."

"You're right, sir. Here, I'll turn them over to you, sir."

Lord Hastings waved the packet away.

"Keep them," he said quietly.

"But—" Jack began.

"Great Scott," Frank put in at this juncture, "you must be getting denser every day, Jack."

Jack wheeled on his chum.

"What do you mean?" he asked.

"Why, can't you see that you are still expected to deliver the papers?"

Jack sank suddenly into a chair.

"Now why didn't I think of that?" he muttered.

"And I suppose, sir," said Frank to Lord Hastings, "that another ship is to be put at Jack's disposal?"

Lord Hastings nodded.

"Exactly," he replied.

Jack was on his feet again immediately.

"What ship, sir?" he asked eagerly.

"The Essex, a sister ship of the Brigadier."

"By George! That's fine, isn't it?" exclaimed Jack.

"And do I go along, sir?" Frank wanted to know.

Again Lord Hastings nodded.

"You do," he replied, "together with the officers and crew of the Brigadier who survived the recent engagement. Your compliment will be filled from other vessels damaged in the raid."

"And where is the Essex now, sir?" asked Jack.

"Here," replied Lord Hastings, "in Dover. You are to go aboard this evening."

"I can't get there too quickly to suit me," declared Jack.

"Same here," Frank agreed.

"Now, remember," enjoined Lord Hastings, "that I still am desirous of your delivering to Secretary Daniels the document I gave you."

"Is the Admiralty still unconvinced of the likelihood of submarines reaching American waters, sir?" asked Frank.

"It is, but you know my opinion has not changed."

"I begin to agree with you, sir," said Jack. "At first I'll admit I was skeptical, but the way you explain the matter it sounds reasonable."

"Well," said Frank, "I hope we get there in time to spoil their plans."

"Amen to that, my boy," said Lord Hastings. "But, I'll detain you no longer. You both probably are anxious to get a look at your new vessel."

"But we have no sailing orders, sir," said Jack.

"You will have before morning," was Lord Hastings reply. "I don't like to hurry you off, but the truth is I'm busy and will have to get down to work."

"Sorry we have detained you so long," said Jack. "Goodbye, sir."

They shook hands all around, and the lads wended their way to the harbor, where they soon were put on board their new ship.

"And now," said Frank, "while we had a good time and all that, I hope this voyage won't be interrupted."

"My sentiments exactly," Jack agreed. "I want to have another look at America."

## CHAPTER XI

## THE WARNING GIVEN

"Land Ho!"

The cry came from the forward lookout, posted aloft.

Jack clapped his binoculars to his eyes and gazed earnestly ahead.

"Where do you make our position, sir?" asked Lieutenant Hetherton.

"Off the Virginia Capes," was Jack's reply. "We should pick up Fort Monroe before noon."

Jack was a good prophet. It still lacked half an hour of midday when the outlines of the historic fortress at Old Point became distinguishable in the distance.

The Essex slipped quietly through the smooth waters of Hampton Roads and dropped anchor some distance off shore. At Jack's command the launch was made ready, and leaving Lieutenant Hetherton in command, Jack motioned Frank to follow him into the launch.

A moment later they were gliding shoreward through the water.

"We'll have to pay our respects to the commandant," said Jack. "It would be a breach of etiquette if we didn't. Also, I want to ascertain the best place to anchor for the next week or so."

"Surely you're not figuring on staying here," protested Frank.

"Not at all, but you know these papers I have been entrusted with must be delivered, and I can't deliver them here. I'll have to go to Washington."

"Right," Frank agreed. "I had forgotten. And are you going to take me along?"

Jack smiled.

"Well, I might, if you are real good," he said.

"I'll be good," Frank promised.

"Hello," said Jack at this point, "if I'm not mistaken, here comes a guard of honor to escort us to the commandant."

Toward the point where the launch now moved, half a dozen American officers approached. They extended helping hands as Jack and Frank scrambled ashore. Jack addressed the senior officer, a major.

"I am Captain Templeton of H.M.S. Essex," he said. "Will you please escort me into the presence of the commandant?"

"With pleasure, sir," replied the major. "Come with me."

He led the way, Frank and the other American officers following. Jack was received immediately by the commandant. Their conference was brief, and soon Jack returned to the place where he had left Frank.

"Well, what did he say?" demanded Frank, as they made their way back toward the launch.

"Said it would be well to continue to Newport News," said Jack. "Docking facilities are better there right now. We can tie up alongside one of the piers there, or anchor off shore, as we choose. Said he would send word of our coming."

"Good," said Frank. "Then I suppose we shall continue without delay?"

"Yes."

"But if memory serves," said Frank, "Newport News is on the James River, and not Hampton Roads."

"Correct," replied Jack.

"Well, I didn't know the river was navigable by a vessel of our draught."

"It is, nevertheless," replied Jack.

They stepped into the launch, and were soon back aboard the Essex. Jack immediately gave the necessary commands and the vessel moved forward.

Two hours later the Essex anchored in the James River half a mile off shore. Frank took in the scene about him, and expressed his wonder.

Shipping of all the allied and many of the neutral nations was to be seen on every hand. Almost over night, it seemed, Newport News had grown from a port of little importance to one of the greatest shipping centers in the United States. There, half a mile away, Frank saw one of the great German merchantmen, which had been interned soon after the outbreak of the war, but which was later to be converted into a United States auxiliary cruiser.

"Well," said Jack, "there is no use delaying here. The commandant at the fort informed me that about the quickest way to get to Washington now is to take a boat up the Potomac."

"And where do we get the boat?" asked Frank.

"Norfolk. But what's the matter with you, Frank? Where's your geography? Seems to me that if I were born and lived most of my life in the United States I would know something about it."

"I do know something about it," declared Frank; "but how do you expect me to know all these details? This is the first time I've ever been in Newport News, and I've never been to Norfolk. How do we get there from here?"

"Either in the Essex's launch, or by ferry."

"Which way do you choose?"

"Ferry, I guess. It will save trouble all around."

"Any way suits me," said Frank.

"You talk like you were dead certain of going along," remarked Jack with a grin.

"Of course I do. I know you could not be hard-hearted enough to leave me behind."

"Nevertheless," Jack declared, "I'm not sure I shouldn't leave you in command here."

"By George! That's no way to talk," declared Frank. "Hetherton can stick on the job here."

"Well, I guess it will be all right," said Jack. "We may as well pack what belongings we shall need. We shouldn't be gone more than a day or two."

"I hope so, and I feel sure we shall. There has been no sign yet of enemy activities in this water."

"And there won't be any sign in advance. When the Germans strike it will be suddenly."

The lads threw what belongings they believed they would need into their handbags and were rowed ashore. They proceeded at once to the pier of the Chesapeake and Ohio ferry and soon were moving along toward Norfolk.

It was a short ride to Norfolk. Arrived in the city an hour later, they inquired the way to the offices of the Washington and Norfolk Steamboat company, where they were fortunate enough to be able to secure a stateroom that night.

It was still early, so the lads spent the afternoon looking about the city, called by the natives the "New York of the South." They went aboard the steamer Northland at 5.30 o'clock, and at 6 the boat left its pier. Jack and Frank remained on deck until after the Northland had put in at Old Point and taken on additional passengers. Then they went below to dinner.

"You know this isn't a bad boat," Frank declared after a walk around, following their dinner.

"Indeed it isn't," Jack agreed. "It has all the comforts of home. It's rather small, but outside of that I can't see anything wrong with it."

"I guess it's big enough for us to-night," grinned Frank.

There were a score or more of American army and navy officers aboard and with some of these the lads struck up an acquaintance. In fact, so interested were some of the Americans in the lads' experiences that they sat up late regaling their newly found friends with accounts of warfare in European waters.

Nevertheless, Jack and Frank were up early the following morning and had a substantial breakfast before the boat docked at the foot of Seventh street in the nation's capital. There they took a taxi and were driven to the Raleigh hotel.

"Now," said Jack, "the first thing to do is to get in touch with the British ambassador and have him arrange an audience with the secretary of the navy at the earliest possible moment."

Jack got the embassy on the telephone, told who he was and announced that he would be on hand to see the ambassador within the hour. Then the lads were driven to the embassy. Here Jack presented his credentials and expressed his desire to see the secretary of the navy at once.

"You return to your hotel," said the ambassador. "I'll arrange the audience and call for you in my automobile."

The lads followed these instructions.

At 2 o'clock in the afternoon the ambassador called for them. They were driven at once to the War and Navy department building on Pennsylvania avenue and were ushered almost immediately to the offices of Secretary Daniels. After a wait of perhaps five minutes, Mr. Daniels' private secretary announced.

"Mr. Daniels will see you now."

The three passed into the secretary's private office, where the British ambassador introduced the lads. Secretary Daniels expressed his pleasure at the meeting, then said:

"And now what can I do for you, gentlemen?"

For answer Jack passed over the papers entrusted him by the Admiralty. Secretary Daniels scanned them briefly.

"These matters shall be attended to, gentlemen," he said. "Now, is there anything else?"

"There is, sir," said Jack, "and a matter probably of much greater importance."

He drew from his pocket the documents given him by Lord Hastings, and these he also passed to Secretary Daniels. The latter read them carefully, his face drawn into a scowl.

"Hm-m-m," he said at last. "Hm-m-m."

He grew silent, apparently lost in thought. At last he spoke.

"I have had some such fears myself," he said at last, "but it seems they are not shared by other officials of the department. I dislike to take matters altogether into my hands, and yet I suppose I can do it. First, however, I shall make an effort to convince my associates through these documents."

"I am instructed to say, sir," said Jack, "that it would be well if you gave the matter prompt attention."

"Oh," said Secretary Daniels, "I anticipate no immediate trouble; and still this is a matter that should not be overlooked. I thank you, gentlemen, for bringing the matter to my attention."

He rose from his chair, signifying that the interview was ended.

Jack and Frank left the Navy department, and the ambassador dropped them at their hotel.

"I don't know what to think of the Secretary of the Navy," said Jack when they were alone. "He didn't seem greatly interested."

"He is the man, you know," said Frank, "who wanted to change the technical terms of port and starboard to right and left."

"That's so," said Jack, "but I'll venture to say he can rise to an emergency."

"There is no doubt about that," Frank agreed, and added quietly: "Americans always have."

## CHAPTER XII

## THE U-BOATS APPEAR

Three weeks passed and Jack and Frank were still in Washington. Immediately after delivering his messages to Secretary Daniels, Jack got in touch with the British Admiralty wireless and asked for instructions. When the reply came it was signed Lord Hastings and said merely:

"Stay where you are pending further orders."

And after three weeks no word had come.

Several times during the three weeks Jack and Frank, or one of the lads at a time, had returned to Newport News to look to the needs of the Essex, which still lay quietly in the James river. Steam was kept up in the destroyer every moment of the day, and she was ready to put to sea on an instant's notice.

"Chances are when we need her it will be in a hurry," said Jack.

Therefore nothing was overlooked that would enable the destroyer to go into action on a moment's notice. Provisions were added to the stores from time to time, and the crew were put through their drills daily.

Meanwhile, from what Jack and Frank learned from the British ambassador, no steps had been taken to prepare for a possible German attack on shipping in American waters. True, the coast defenses had been strengthened, but that was merely a matter of routine for a country at war.

Off the coast, warships were on patrol. But there were comparatively few of these, for the bulk of the American fleet had been sent abroad to reinforce the British grand fleet patroling the North Sea.

Jack and Frank discussed these matters frequently.

"It would be a great time for the Germans to strike," said Jack one evening, as the lads sat in their rooms at the hotel. "The American people don't seem to realize the possibilities of the submarine."

"That's true," said Frank, "but at the same time such an attack might prove a boomerang to the Germans."

"What do you mean?"

"Why," said Frank, "you haven't forgotten, have you, that it took a number of air raids on England to fully arouse the British people to the fact that the Germans must be licked?"

"That's true enough," agreed Jack. "The Germans, of course, figured that they would frighten England and scare her out of the war."

"Exactly, and the result was altogether different from what they had anticipated. That's why I say submarine activities off the American coast will prove a boomerang to the foe."

"I see," commented Jack. "You mean it would arouse the American people to the necessity of prompt action."

"Exactly."

"Well," said Jack, "it begins to look as though Lord Hastings were wrong. We've been here three weeks now and nothing has transpired to indicate that the Germans are meditating a submarine raid in American waters."

"You don't expect them to tip the Washington government off in advance, do you?" asked Frank with a laugh.

"Hardly; but it would seem that if such a campaign had been planned it would have been started before this."

"It wouldn't surprise me," said Frank, "to get a flash any day that a ship had been submarined off the American coast."

Came a rap at the door.

"Come in," Frank called.

A bell boy entered. He held a tray in his hand and on the tray was a cablegram.

"From Lord Hastings, I suppose," said Frank, taking the message and passing it to Jack.

Jack broke the seal, spread out the paper. The message, in code, was this:

"Authentic information flotilla submarines headed for America. Warn Navy Department at once."

Jack sprang to the telephone and got the British embassy on the wire.

"The ambassador, quick!" he said to the voice that answered his call.

There was a short pause, and then Jack recognized the ambassador's voice.

"I've just had a wireless from Lord Hastings relative to the matter which we discussed with Secretary Daniels several weeks ago," he explained. "Can you arrange another interview immediately?"

"I'll see," said the ambassador and rang off.

The telephone in the lads' room jangled sharply ten minutes later. Jack sprang to the wire.

"Yes," he said in response to a query. "Ten o'clock? You'll call for us? Very well."

He replaced the receiver and turned to Frank.

"We will see Secretary Daniels in his office at ten," he said. He looked at his watch. "Hurry and dress. It's after nine now. The ambassador should be here in fifteen minutes."

The lads jumped into their clothes, then went downstairs, where they awaited the arrival of the ambassador. The latter arrived ten minutes before ten o'clock, and the three were driven to the War and Navy building. Secretary Daniels received them at once.

"I understand that you come on a very important matter," he said. "Pray, what is it, gentlemen?"

For answer Jack laid before the American naval secretary the decoded message from Lord Hastings. The secretary read it, then looked up.

"Well?" he asked.

"Why, sir," said Jack, "Lord Hastings simply wishes you to take all precautions to prevent sinking of vessels by submarines in American waters."

Secretary Daniels smiled.

"I don't know what we can do that has not already been done," he replied. "The off-coast waters are mined, and American warships are patroling the regular channels of navigation."

"All that may be true, sir," said Jack, "but these submarines are slippery customers, as I have reason to know. It would be well to take even further precautions."

"And what would you suggest?" asked Secretary Daniels.

"Why, sir," said Jack, "I'd suggest cancelling sailing orders of all transports temporarily, at least until such time as I felt sure they could go in safety. Then I'd flash a warning broadcast to all vessels within reach of the wireless to be on the lookout for enemy submarines. I'd rush every available submarine chaser in the Atlantic ports beyond the mine fields and I would order a destroyer as protection for every vessel known to be inward bound."

Secretary Daniels smiled.

"You wouldn't overlook anything, would you, Captain?"

"I certainly would not," said Jack firmly.

"Very well, then," said Secretary Daniels. "I'll set your mind at rest. Your suggestions shall be followed out. I'll give the necessary directions the first thing in the morning."

"In the morning, sir?" repeated Jack. "The morning may be too late."

"Oh, I guess not," Secretary Daniels smiled. "It has been three weeks or more since your first warning and nothing has happened. I guess we can safely depend upon being let alone a few hours after the second warning."

Jack was about to protest, thought better of it and said simply:

"Very well, sir."

A moment later the lads took their departure with the ambassador. In the seclusion of the latter's automobile, Jack said:

"I can't see how the secretary dares let time slip by like that."

"Never mind," said the ambassador, "you'll find in a day or two that Secretary Daniels knows what he's doing. Don't make any mistake about him. He's a capable man."

"I have no doubt of that, sir," replied Jack. "But if he had seen three years of war, as we have, he would never delay. Besides, he doesn't know these German submarines as well as I do. Neither do any of the Americans."

"Oh, yes they do," declared Frank.

"They do, eh?" exclaimed Jack. "Well, I'd like to know the name of one of them."

"His name," said Frank, "is Lieutenant Chadwick, and I think he knows just about as much about the U-Boats as you do; and he agrees with your ideas perfectly."

Jack smiled.

"That's right," he said. "I had forgotten you were a native of this land. Well, here's hoping nothing happens before Secretary Daniels takes all necessary precautions."

The British ambassador left the lads at their hotel, and they returned at once to their rooms, where for several hours they discussed the situation.

"There is no use talking about it," said Frank at last. "Let's go to bed."

They undressed.

Just before extinguishing the light, as was his custom, Frank raised the window. As he looked out he saw below a crowd of excited men and women moving about the street.

"Hey, Jack!" he called. "Come here."

Jack joined him at the window.

"Now what's up, do you suppose?" asked Frank.

"Too deep for me," declared Jack, "but something surely. Let's go down and find out."

Hurriedly they slipped back into their clothes, and went down stairs. They stepped out of the hotel and mingled with the people on the streets, quite a crowd for Washington at that hour of the night.

The stream of people led toward Eleventh and Pennsylvania avenue, where a larger crowd was gathered in front of a bulletin board in the window of a newspaper office.

"Big news of some kind," said Jack as they hurried along.

"And not good news, either," Frank declared. "There'd be some cheering if it were."

"You're right," said Jack.

By main force they wormed their way through the crowd, until they were close enough to read the bulletin board. Then Jack uttered an exclamation of alarm.

"I knew it!" he cried.

For what he read was this:

"Navy Department announces sinking of two freight vessels off New Jersey coast by German submarines."

"I knew it!" Jack said again.

## CHAPTER XIII

## THE SUBMARINES GROW BOLDER

The boys returned to their rooms.

"Now what?" asked Frank.

"I don't know," was Jack's reply. "I hate to sit here quietly when the whole American navy, or what part of it is still here, is in chase of the Germans, but what are we going to do about it?"

"Search me," replied Frank.

"Our instructions," Jack continued, "are to stay here pending further orders."

"Maybe we'll get them soon," said Frank.

"Yes; and maybe we won't."

"Then we'll just have to sit tight."

"That's what worries me."

There was a knock at the door.

"Come in," Frank called.

A bell boy entered with a second cablegram.

Jack tore it open hastily.

"Hurray!" he cried.

"What's up?" demanded Frank.

He arose and peered over his chum's shoulder. What he read was this:

"Offer your services and the services of the Essex to the U.S. Navy Department at once."

"Fine!" cried Frank. "Let's get busy."

It was the work of half an hour, however, to get Secretary Daniels on the telephone. He had been aroused at the first news of the sinkings off the coast and had been kept on the jump ever since. But he took time to talk to Jack.

"I am authorized by the British Admiralty, sir," said Jack over the 'phone, "to offer the services of my ship to the American government."

"Accepted with thanks," snapped Secretary Daniels. "You will proceed immediately to your vessel in Newport News, after which you will join the American vessels on patrol duty off the coast of Virginia. I shall inform Admiral Sellings that you will report to him for instructions."

Without awaiting a reply, Secretary Daniels hung up.

"By George!" said Jack. "He's a man of action when he gets to moving."

"What did he say?" demanded Frank.

"Hurry and pack your things," was Jack's reply. "I'll explain as we work."

It was the work of only a few minutes for the lads to gather their belongings and dump them in their handbags. Then they hurried downstairs, where they paid their bill and learned that they could catch a train to Richmond within the hour.

"Going after the submarines?" asked the night clerk.

"Yes," replied Jack shortly.

"Good! I hope you get 'em. Here's your taxi."

The lads jumped into the taxi and were driven to the station, where they caught their train with time to spare.

It lacked two hours of daylight when they arrived in Richmond. They took a taxi across town to the Chesapeake and Ohio station, where they caught a train for Newport News an hour later. At eight o'clock they were in Newport News, and fifteen minutes later stepped aboard the Essex.

"Glad to see you back, sir," said Lieutenant Hetherton, who held the deck. "I suppose you've heard — — "

"Pipe all hands to quarters, Mr. Hetherton," Jack interrupted sharply, "and clear ship for action. We sail within the hour."

Lieutenant Hetherton hurried away.

"Frank," said Jack, "go below and have a look at the engine room. Then find the quartermaster and see about provisions and fuel."

Frank also hurried away.

Sailing preparations aboard the Essex were made hurriedly and within less than an hour all was ready for departure. Meanwhile, crowds had collected ashore, upon learning that the Essex was about to set out in pursuit of the German undersea raiders.

Loud cheers split the air. Men and women waved their handkerchiefs. From a group of soldiers on the shore came expressions of good luck. In response to Jack's request, a pilot had been hurried aboard and now took the wheel.

"Half speed ahead," Jack ordered.

The water churned up ahead of the Essex, and she moved majestically toward the center of the stream.

Gradually the cheering died away in the distance, and the city of Newport News was lost to sight. In Hampton Roads again, the pilot was dropped in a small boat and rowed shoreward.

Frank took his place behind the helmsman and Jack rang for full speed ahead. At last the Essex was off in pursuit of the German submarines.

Meanwhile, an account of the activity of the enemy off the coats is in order. Besides the sinking of the first two freight vessels, which had been reported to the Navy Department by survivors who had reached shore in small boats, other vessels had been sent to the bottom. Most of these were freighters or small trading ships, including two sailing vessels. Some had been sunk off the New Jersey coast, others off the coasts of Delaware and Virginia.

In some cases the vessels attacked had attempted to flee, but they were quickly overhauled by the submarines, which, besides firing torpedoes into their hulls, shelled them with rapid fire guns and later attacked the small boats in which the crews sought to make the shore.

Casualties had been heavy aboard the ships sunk by the raiders. One or two of the enemy submarines had been fired on by armed ships, but to no avail; and as a result of those efforts, the death lists aboard such vessels had been increased, for the Germans, angered, had swept the survivors in small boats with rapid fire guns.

How many submarines were operating in American waters, the Navy department did not know. From the fact that ships were attacked in at least three places, within a short space of time, however, it was believed that there were at least three or four of the raiders.

From all ports along the coast, destroyers, submarine chasers, motor boats armed with single guns, had put to sea in an effort to run down the raiders. But off the New Jersey coast, almost in the midst of these vessels, a sailing ship was sunk by a submarine. Before any of the patroling vessels could reach the scene, however, the U-Boat had submerged and fled.

Depth bombs were dropped by ships of war wherever it was thought a submarine might be lurking beneath the water. But these efforts met with no success. Reports of sinkings in other parts of the water reached the Navy department.

The first sinking was reported on May 10. In the week that followed, eighteen other vessels were sent to the bottom by German submarines off the American coast. At the end of that time, however, the waters were being so well patrolled that it would have been suicide for a submarine to have showed itself.

Reports of sinkings ceased. But, from time to time, word was received that submarines had been sighted farther south, first off the coast of the Carolinas and then off Florida. No attacks were made in these waters, however, and the next that was heard of the submarines they were off the coast of South America.

During the activities of the enemy raiders, one submarine was sunk, and one was captured, both through the efforts of Jack and the crew and officers of the Essex.

After leaving Hampton Roads, the Essex steamed out beyond the Virginia Capes. Immediately Jack sought to get into communication with Admiral Sellings by wireless. And at last he raised the admiral's flagship, the Dakota.

"What do you want?" came the query from the Dakota, after Jack's flash had been picked up.

"British destroyer Essex, Captain Templeton, reporting to Admiral Sellings for orders at the request of Secretary Daniels," was the message Jack sent back.

"One moment," was the reply.

Jack waited in the radio room aboard the Essex.

"Essex! Essex!" came the call five minutes later.

"Answer," Jack directed the operator.

"Essex replying," the operator flashed.

"Admiral Sellings orders Essex to proceed north and stand out to sea to protect inbound vessels. Understand one submarine sighted five miles out five hours ago. Repeat."

The operator repeated the message to show that he had caught in correctly.

Jack went on deck and gave instructions necessary to putting the Essex out at sea. Then, "Full speed ahead!" he signalled.

The British destroyer Essex stood out to sea magnificently. Aboard, her crew stood to their posts, ready for action. Jack, surrounded by his officers, held the bridge.

"We've got to keep a sharp eye out," said Jack.

"Right," Frank agreed. "We're likely to come upon one of the enemy any moment, and we can't afford to let him see us first."

"Very true, sir," Lieutenant Hetherton agreed. "Fortunately all our lookouts have sharp eyes. I'll venture to say a submarine won't come to the surface very close to us without being seen."

"That's the way to talk, Mr. Hetherton," said Jack. "It shows the proper spirit."

"And the men are imbued with the same spirit," declared Frank, "and yet see how cool they are."

It was perfectly true. There was no confusion aboard the Essex in spite of the fact that each member of the crew knew he was bent on a dangerous mission. One shot from the submarine, they knew, if truly aimed and Jack was unable to maneuver the vessel out of harm's way, would be the end. However, like all British tars, they had absolute confidence in their commander; for, according to their line of reasoning, if he were not a capable officer and to be depended upon he would not be in command of the ship.

Suddenly the radio operator appeared on deck and hurried toward the bridge. Jack stepped forward to meet him. The lad took the message the operator passed him and read:

"S.O.S. Pursued by submarine eighteen miles off Cape May light. Am running south by west, but foe is gaining. Capt. Griswold, Ventura."

"This," said Jack quietly, "means that there is still another U-Boat to be reckoned with, but I had no idea they were operating so far out. We'll have to get busy."

Jack looked at his officers with a slight smile on his face, then ordered: "Shape your course due east, Frank. Full speed ahead."

## CHAPTER XIV

## THE U-87

As the Essex sped forward the radio operator from time to time picked up other messages from the Ventura.

"She's headed directly toward us," Jack explained to Frank. "We should sight her within the hour."

The Ventura was sighted in less, but under peculiar conditions.

"Ship on the starboard bow, sir," sang the lookout forward.

A moment later the officers on the bridge sighted the vessel through their glasses.

"By George! She seems to be standing still," said Frank.

"So she does," Lieutenant Hetherton agreed, "Wonder what's the matter?"

"We'll find out fast enough," returned Jack quietly.

"Take the bridge, Mr. Chadwick," said Jack. "I'm going below to the radio room."

"See if you can raise the Ventura," he instructed the radio operator, a few moments later.

"Ventura! Ventura!" went the call through the air.

There was no response.

"Try it again," said Jack.

The operator obeyed. Still there was no reply from the Ventura.

"Something wrong," Jack muttered under his breath, "and still I saw no sign of a submarine. Try 'em again, Wilkins."

Again the radio operator sent the call flashing through the air:

"Ventura! Ventura! Ventura!"

The instrument at Wilkins' side began to click.

"Ventura replying, sir," Wilkins reported.

"I hear him," said Jack briefly. "Let me get at that key, Wilkins."

The operator sprang up and Jack took his place and strapped the receiver over his head.

"What's the trouble, Ventura?" he clicked.

"Held up by submarine," was the reply. "U-Boat due east of us. You can't see her. We sighted you just after we were boarded."

"Then how does it come you are at the key?" Jack clicked.

"Broke away from captors on deck. They are pounding at the door now."

"Have they sighted us?"

"They hadn't. There goes the door, Good-bye."

The flashes from the Ventura ceased. Jack sprang up and turned the receiver over to the operator.

"Keep calling," he said. "If you pick the Ventura up again, let me know. I'll send a man so you can report to me through him."

Jack hurried on deck.

In the distance the Ventura was plainly visible now. Jack changed the course of the ship slightly, and after the vessel had gone half a mile he made out the form of a submarine lying close astern of the Ventura.

"By George! They must see us," he muttered. "If the lookout on the U-Boat hasn't espied us, surely some of the Germans on the deck of the Ventura must have done so. Wonder why the submarine captain doesn't sink the steamer and submerge. Surely he is not going to risk an encounter with me."

Nevertheless, it seemed that such must be the submarine commander's intention, for the submarine showed no sign of submerging as the Essex bore down on her.

Through his binoculars Frank was now able to ascertain the fact that a struggle was in progress on the deck of the Ventura. A dozen or more figures, closely interlocked, were scuffling to and fro across the bridge. Frank gave an exclamation.

"I know what's wrong," he ejaculated.

"Well, what?" demanded Jack, turning to him.

"Why, the crew, or some of the crew, has jumped the commander of the submarine and his escort. That's why the officer left on the U-Boat doesn't dare sink the vessel. And the crew of the steamer is keeping the German and his friends so busy aboard that they haven't had a chance to jump overboard."

"By George! I guess you're right," declared Jack. "Now if they can hold them fifteen minutes longer we'll get in the game ourselves."

Again Jack altered the course of the Essex and approached the submarine at an angle from the Ventura.

"Forward turret guns there!" he roared.

It was the signal the men had been eagerly awaiting. Quickly the signal "ready" was flashed in the forward turret. The men were already at their posts.

"Range finders!" ordered Jack.

"Aye, aye, sir," came the reply of the officer in charge of this work, and he calculated the range swiftly and passed the word to the captain of the gun crew in the forward turret.

"Fire!"

A heavy shell flew screaming across the water.

But the range had not been correct and the shell flew past the submarine. Again the range was calculated, taking into consideration the first error. Again the command to fire was given.

This time the range had been gauged perfectly and the shell must have gone home had it not been for one thing.

A moment before the command to fire was given, a torpedo was launched by the submarine. Jack saw the torpedo come dashing through the water, and he was forced to order the helm over promptly to escape the deadly messenger. This maneuver was made at the precise moment that the Essex fired for the second time, and consequently the shell again went wide.

Almost at the same instant Frank, who had kept his eyes glued to the deck of the Ventura where the struggle on the bridge had continued fiercely, uttered an exclamation of alarm.

"They've broken away," he cried.

It was true, The submarine commander and his followers had succeeded in eluding the crew of the Ventura and dashed to the rail. There they poised themselves a brief moment, and then flung themselves headlong into the sea. Directly, dripping, they appeared on the deck of the submarine and dashed for the conning tower.

"Quick!" roared Jack. "Forward turret guns again there!"

Once more the range was calculated and an explosion shook the Essex. But as before the range had not been true. The shell barely skimmed the top of the U-Boat and went screaming half a mile past, where it struck the water with a hiss.

Slowly the submarine began to submerge.

"Again!" cried Jack.

But the next shot had no better success.

The submarine disappeared from sight.

Jack stamped his foot.

"What's the matter with those fellows forward?" he demanded. "Can't they shoot? Didn't they ever see a gun before?"

There was no reply from the other officers and gradually Jack cooled down.

"Pretty tough," said Frank then. "We should have had that fellow."

Jack nodded gloomily.

"So we should," he cried, "but we didn't get him. Well, better luck next time. All the same, I'm inclined to believe that Ensign Carruthers needs a talking to. He didn't take the time to calculate the range correctly."

"I'll speak to him," said Frank.

"Do," said Jack. "In the meantime we'll run close to the Ventura and I'll go aboard for a word with her captain."

The Ventura's wireless was working again now, and Jack himself took the key.

"Lay to," he ordered. "I'm coming aboard you."

"Very well," was the reply.

The two vessels drew close together. Jack had the destroyer's launch lowered, climbed in and crossed to the Ventura, where a ladder was lowered for him. On deck he was greeted by a grizzled old sailor, who introduced himself as Captain Griswold.

"Come to my cabin, sir," he said to Jack. "We can talk there without being interrupted."

Jack followed the captain of the Ventura below, and took a seat the latter motioned him to. The captain set out liquor and cigars, but Jack waved them away.

"I neither smoke nor drink, thanks," he said.

Captain Griswold shrugged his shoulders and put a match to a cigar.

"Well, what can I do for you, Captain?" he asked.

"First," said Jack, "did you get the number of the submarine?"

"I did. The U-87, Commander Frederich, the captain styled himself; and if there ever was a murderer unhung, he's the man."

"Why?" asked Jack curiously.

"Because he proposed setting my passengers and crew adrift in small boats, without water or provisions, before sinking my ship. And when I told him that I had him figured correctly—that he intended to shell the lifeboats—the cold-blooded scoundrel admitted it! That's why we had the nerve to jump him on deck. I figured we might as well die on the Ventura as in the lifeboats—and we had a chance of taking him to Davy Jones' locker along with us."

"I see," said Jack. "Not a bad idea."

"It was offered by the wireless operator," continued Captain Griswold, "although he offered it unconsciously."

"Explain," Jack requested.

"Well, Harrington thought he heard his instrument clicking. He figured it was you, whom we had just sighted. He broke through the Germans on deck and dashed below. He locked himself in his room and began talking to you. Three of the enemy went after him and broke in the door, but I guess he had told you enough by that time."

"I'd like a word with this Harrington," said Jack. "He is a brave man. Where is he?"

"Dead," said Captain Griswold quietly.

Jack jumped to his feet

"Dead?" he repeated.

"Yes. After the Germans broke in the door, they overpowered him, tied him and then brought back on deck. Said the German commander: 'I'll show you how we treat men who defy us.' He stepped back several paces, drew his revolver and fired. Then three of the enemy threw the body into the sea. That's when we jumped them, for it was more than we could stand."

"Then who answered the wireless when I called a moment ago?"

"I did."

"I guess that is enough, Captain," said Jack. He returned to the Essex.

## CHAPTER XV

## JACK GIVES CHASE

"Any sight of the submarine, Frank?" asked Jack, when he stepped on deck again.

"None," was the reply. "In accordance with instructions you gave before you went overside we dropped depth bombs in the spot where the U-Boat disappeared, but without result."

"I guess he's gone, then," said Jack. "But I'd like to get my hands on that fellow," and he related to Frank the manner in which the German commander had shot down the wireless operator aboard the Ventura.

"By Jove! What a murderous scoundrel!" muttered Frank.

Jack nodded.

"No worse than the rest of them, I'll wager," he said. "But, hello! The Ventura's moving again."

As soon as Jack had left the deck of the steamer, Captain Griswold had ordered the engines started and prepared for a quick dash to shore.

"There are likely to be more of those pesky submarines about here," he muttered, "and the sooner I reach port the better."

Accordingly he ordered full speed ahead.

"Do you know," said Frank, "I've a hunch that the U-87 is not through with the Ventura. You know how the German is. He doesn't like to admit he's been licked, so I figure the submarine commander is likely to have gone ahead and will be awaiting the approach of the Ventura."

"Now by George! I wouldn't be a bit surprised," Jack agreed. "Well, we'll be ready for him."

"What are you going to do, Jack?"

"I'll show you. Come."

Jack dashed to the radio room, Frank at his heels.

"Get the Ventura for me," Jack instructed the operator.

It was perhaps five minutes later that the Ventura answered the call. Jack took the key.

"Captain Griswold?" he asked.

"Yes. Who are you?"

"Captain Templeton, destroyer Essex."

"Well, what do you want this time?"

"Slow down. I'm coming aboard again."

"What for?"

"I'll explain when I get there."

"All right, but I'll tell you I don't like this business."

The instrument became silent.

"Now tell me what you're going to do, Jack," said Frank, as he followed his chum and commander on deck.

"It's very simple," said Jack. "As you have said, I believe that the submarine commander will intercept the Ventura again farther along toward the shore. Now, I'm going to turn the Essex over to you temporarily and go aboard the Ventura. You know the Germans as well as I do. This man will no more think of sinking the Ventura without doing a bit of bragging to the captain, who fooled him once, than he will of flying."

"That's true enough," Frank admitted.

"All right. Now I'll be aboard when he gets there. If he comes aboard, I'll grab him there. If he doesn't I'll jump to the deck of the submarine after him and tumble him overboard. I'll trust to you to keep the submarine occupied and to get a boat to me."

"It's a desperate venture, Jack," Frank protested.

"So it is," was Jack's reply, "but I've a longing to capture this fellow. If we just sink the submarine, I can't do it of course. Another thing, it may be that I am not doing just right in leaving my ship, but it will only be for a couple of hours and I know you can handle it as well as I can."

"Oh, I won't sink her," grinned Frank. "But why not let me be the one to go?"

"Because I'm not sure you can handle the German commander."

"But you're sure you can, eh?"

"He'll have to be something new in the line of a German if I can't."

"All right," said Frank. "Have it your own way. You're boss here, you know."

Meantime the Essex and the Ventura had been drawing closer together. Directly a boat put off from the destroyer and ran alongside of the steamer. Jack clambered over the side and the launch returned to the destroyer.

Captain Griswold was waiting for Jack.

"Now what's up?" he wanted to know.

"Come to your cabin and I'll explain," said Jack.

In the seclusion of the cabin he outlined the situation. When he had concluded a sketch of his plans, Captain Griswold demurred.

"But I don't like to risk my passengers," he said.

"You won't be risking them any more with me aboard than you will without me," Jack explained. "Besides, you will have the additional protection of the destroyer. In fact, it may be that the presence of the Essex will scare the submarine off, but I doubt it. The German commander, as all of his ilk, is angry at having been balked of his prey. He'll probably have one more try, destroyer or no destroyer."

"Well," said Captain Griswold, "you're a British naval officer and should know something, whether you do or not. But I'll tell you right now I hope the submarine doesn't show up again."

Nevertheless, Captain Griswold was doomed to disappointment, for the U-87 did reappear.

It was almost 6 o'clock in the evening when all on board were startled by a cry from the lookout.

"Submarine on the port bow, sir."

Instantly all became confusion on the big merchant ship. Passengers, of whom there were perhaps fifty, became greatly excited. Every man on board strapped on a life preserver, and waited for he knew not what.

The fact that, directly astern, the Essex, British destroyer, was in plain sight and trailing them, did not allay their fears. Came a shot from a gun mounted forward on the submarine, a signal to heave to.

"Obey it," said Jack, to Captain Griswold, on the bridge.

Captain Griswold ordered his engines stopped.

"I'll keep out of sight for a moment," said Jack. "The commander may come on board."

He stooped down in the shelter of the pilot house.

The submarine drew close to the Ventura, and a voice hailed Captain Griswold:

"Thought you'd get away did you, you Yankee pig."

It was the voice of the German commander.

"Oh, we may get away yet," said Captain Griswold.

"Don't depend on the destroyer this time," shouted the commander of the submarine. "I see her approaching, but she won't be soon enough. I'll sink you and submerge before she can fire a shot."

"Well, you big cut throat," shouted Captain Griswold, losing his temper, "why don't you do it?"

"You dare to talk to a German officer like that?" thundered the submarine commander. "You shall be sunk immediately. But first I wanted a word with you. I just wanted to tell you what fate I hold in store for you."

"It's my opinion," said Captain Griswold, "that you're a big bluff, like all the rest of your stripe."

Meantime, realizing that the German commander did not intend to board the Ventura a second time, Jack crept from the shelter of the pilot house unobserved and stole across the deck until he was beside the rail just above the U-Boat, whose sides almost scraped the Ventura, so close were the two vessels together.

Jack removed his coat and his cap, which he dropped on deck. Then he stood up in full view of the German submarine commander. The latter gazed at him carelessly, for without his cap and coat Jack showed no sign of being a British naval officer.

Jack took in the scene about him with a careful eye. The German commander stood close to the conning tower. There were perhaps half a dozen men beside him, presumably his officers. The commander was directly below the spot where Jack stood.

One of the Germans, Jack noticed, kept a close eye on the approaching Essex and from time to time spoke to the commander in a low tone.

"Oh, these English can't shoot," Jack heard the commander say at last. "However, I guess we have delayed long enough. Inside with you, gentlemen."

Two of the Germans descended through the conning tower. This left four on the deck of the submarine besides the commander. These, too, moved toward the conning tower.

"Guess it's time to get busy," Jack muttered.

With a single movement he leaped to the rail of the Ventura, and with a second hurled himself to the deck of the submarine, landing in the midst of the startled Germans.

At the same moment, Captain Griswold, on the Ventura, signalled his engine room for full speed ahead in accordance with Jack's instructions.

The reason for this was obvious. First, it would take the steamer out of the way of the torpedoes already trained on her, which would not be launched without a command from one of the enemy officers, and, second, it would draw the Ventura away so as to present the submarine as a clear target for the guns of the approaching Essex.

Jack, on the deck of the submarine, recovered himself before the German officers could get over their surprise. He sprang to his feet and waded into them, striking out right and left.

Two men went staggering across the narrow deck and toppled into the sea. The others reached for their revolvers. Before they could fire, however, Jack sprang forward quickly and floored one of the enemy with a smashing blow. This left the commander and one other officer on deck.

The commander fired at Jack, but in his haste the bullet went wild. Jack hurled himself forward, and the men gave ground. One, retreating, lost his balance and went staggering across the deck and fell overboard.

Only the commander of the submarine now faced Jack, and he covered the lad with a revolver.

"Hands up!" he said.

For answer Jack smiled slightly, and took a quick step forward.

"Crack!" the German's revolver spoke sharply, and Jack felt a hot pain in his left arm. But the German had no time to fire again, for Jack was upon him, pinning his revolver arm to his side.

"Now," said the lad, "I've got you!"

The two wrestled across the deck.

## CHAPTER XVI

### THE FIGHT ON THE U-87

In the meantime, members of the crew hearing the commotion on deck, rushed up to see what was going on. Seeing their commander struggling with an enemy, they hurried across the deck.

Jack saw them coming out of the tail of his eye. It was not time to hesitate and the lad knew it.

With his arms still wrapped about the German commander, Jack struggled to the rail and leaped into the sea. Down and down he went, never for a moment relaxing his hold on the German. Then they came to the surface.

With a sudden jerk the German freed himself and aimed a heavy blow at Jack. This Jack dodged and sought to regain his hold on his foe. But the German wriggled away and struck out for the submarine.

In the meantime, Captain Griswold of the Ventura had been watching the struggle as his vessel sped away from the scene. There was a strange light in his eyes and he muttered to himself. At last he muttered an imprecation.

"He's a brave boy," he said. "I can't run away and leave him like that."

He brought the head of the vessel around in spite of the protests of some of the passengers, and headed back for the submarine.

"Man the forward gun there!" he cried.

For the Ventura, like other allied ships plying in the seas in those days, carried small guns for defensive purposes. The gun crew sprang to obey this order and the gun was trained on the submarine.

"Fire!" shouted Captain Griswold.

"Crash!"

The gun spoke and a geyser of water was kicked up just beyond the submarine.

At this point the officer left in command of the submarine seemed to realize his own danger. He sprang to the conning tower, unmindful of the fact that his commander was struggling in the water.

"Down, men!" he cried.

But it appeared that the German sailors were made of sterner stuff than was the officer. They refused to go below until their commander had been brought safely aboard. In vain the officer pointed out their danger.

Jack struck out after the German commander as the latter swam for the submarine. The lad was a powerful swimmer and he felt confident he could overtake the man before help could reach him.

The destroyer Essex had now drawn close. Frank had been afraid to order a shot at the submarine for fear the shell might hit Jack in the water.

"Take the bridge, Mr. Hetherton!" he cried. "Lower a boat, men!"

The boat was lowered in a trice and Frank and a score of sailors sprang in. The launch darted toward Jack at full speed, Frank standing erect and with the quartermaster at the rudder.

They were close enough to see the struggle between Jack and the German commander in the water. Frank saw the man break loose from Jack and strike out for the submarine. He saw Jack make after him, and he saw something more.

Half a dozen German sailors leaped into the water and made for Jack, who apparently did not realize his own danger, so interested was he in the pursuit of the German commander.

"Faster!" cried Frank, and drew his revolver.

Now, for the first time, Jack realized his danger. But it was too late to draw back, and it is doubtful if he would have done so anyway.

"I'm going to get that fellow," he gritted between his teeth, referring to the German commander.

One of the German sailors struck at the lad with a knife. Jack caught the man's arm with his left hand and twisted sharply. There was a snap, and the knife dropped into the water. The sailor uttered a cry of pain and turning, struck out for the submarine with his good arm.

Two sailors now beset Jack on either side, and the German commander turned to renew the struggle.

"Kill him!" he cried angrily.

One of the sailors raised himself high in the water, and a knife flashed above him.

"Crack!"

A revolver spoke sharply and the knife dropped from limp fingers.

Frank, standing erect in the Essex's launch, had fired. Now, as has been said, Frank was a crack shot, and in spite of the pitching of the small boat, his aim had been true. The bullet had struck the German sailor's arm just below the elbow, shattering the nerve.

Perceiving the approach of reinforcements, at an order from their commander, the Germans turned and swam rapidly toward the submarine. The sailors reached the vessel and climbed aboard. Their commander did likewise.

Unmindful of the cries of his friends behind him, Jack also laid hold of the edge of the submarine and drew himself, dripping, aboard the vessel. A sailor near the conning tower raised his revolver in deliberate aim.

"Crack! Crack!"

Two revolvers spoke almost as one, the first Frank's, the second that of the sailor who aimed at Jack. But Frank's bullet went home, thus deflecting the aim of the man who covered Jack, and the German's bullet went wild.

The commander of the submarine, at this juncture, losing his temper at being pursued to the very door of safety, turned and sprang for Jack with a wild cry. He was a big and powerful man, and as he wrapped his arms about Jack, the lad staggered back.

But he recovered his balance in a moment and struck out with his right fist. Struck in the stomach, the German grunted and stepped back.

Now the remainder of the German crew came pouring on deck. At the same time Frank's launch grated alongside and his men poured a volley of rifle bullets into the enemy. The latter turned and scampered for safety below decks.

Jack, still struggling with the German commander, paused and looked around long enough to cry:

"After them, Frank! Don't let them shut you out."

Frank understood and led his men toward the conning tower at a run. Most of the enemy were already inside and descending, but Frank arrived in time to prevent the closing of the conning tower, which would have permitted the submarine to submerge, leaving the struggling figures in the water. With the conning tower open, it was, of course, impossible for the U-Boat to submerge, for she would have been flooded immediately.

Frank's men made prisoners of the half a dozen Germans who had not time to get below, and then the lad ran over to help Jack.

"Keep away, Frank," said Jack. "I've got this fellow, and I hope he doesn't give up too easily. We've heavy accounts to settle with him."

The big German showed no symptoms of giving up. He lashed out with both arms and Jack was kept busy warding off the blows. But the German commander was a novice at this sort of fighting, while Jack, only a year or so before, had won the heavyweight boxing championship of the British navy. So there was no doubt in Frank's mind as to the outcome. He and his men formed a circle around the struggling figures, at the same time guarding the conning tower to prevent the enemy from closing it.

"Shoot the first head you see down there," Frank enjoined the men he left on guard, and he knew they would be only too glad to obey this order.

Jack, with a smile still on his face, permitted the German commander to waste his energy in ineffective blows. Then Jack stepped forward and delivered a heavy blow to the man's mouth. The German staggered back. Jack doubled him up with a left-handed punch to the pit of the stomach, then straightened him with a second hard right to the point of the chin.

The German commander reeled backward. Jack followed up his advantage, and for the space of a minute played a tattoo on the man's face with both fists. Then he stepped back, and as the German came toward him, the lad muttered:

"I guess this has gone far enough. Now for the finish."

He started a blow almost from the deck, and putting his full force behind it, struck.

"Crack!"

The blow could be heard even aboard the Ventura, which had approached close by this time.

The German commander seemed to stagger back all of ten paces, the British sailors scurrying back to keep out of his way. Then the man fell, his head striking the deck with a sickening thud.

"There," said Jack, "I guess that will settle you. Tie him up, men."

A wild cheer had burst from the sailors as Jack delivered the finishing touch. None of these men had ever seen Jack in action before, and it was only natural that they should be greatly impressed at this exhibition of their commander's prowess.

"By glory! What a blow!" one of them exclaimed. "Did you see it, Tom?"

"Did I?" exclaimed the man addressed as Tom; "did I? I'll say I did, and I thought I was pretty handy with my fists. But not against Captain Jack, not for me."

As bidden by Jack, the sailors rolled the German commander over and bound him. Then they carried him to the Essex's launch and threw him in, none too gently, either, for there was no man there who had not a disgust for Germans, German tactics and everything German.

"Now," said Frank to Jack, "I guess we may as well stand clear and let the Essex pour a few shells into the vessel, eh?"

Jack shook his head.

"No," he said, "we shall take possession of the vessel. Call down below and see if the Germans will surrender."

Frank approached the conning tower and called down.

"Hello!" he shouted.

There was no response.

"Hello below!" he shouted again in German.

"What do you want?" came a sullen voice from below.

"We're in possession of this vessel now," said Frank. "Come up here and surrender."

"We'll stay where we are," came the reply after a brief pause.

"But you can't man," exclaimed Frank. "Don't you know when you have been captured."

"We'll stay here awhile," said the spokesman of the sailors.

"But you can't stay there forever, and you can't submerge," said Frank. "Come up and surrender."

To this the lad received no response. Frank reported to Jack.

"So they won't surrender, eh?" said Jack. "Then we'll go down and get them."

"Rather risky, Jack," Frank warned.

"So it is," Jack agreed. "So's the whole war. But wait. We'll see."

## CHAPTER XVII

## CAPTURE OF THE SUBMARINE

Captain Griwsold aboard the Ventura had watched the struggle on the submarine with eager eyes. His fingers clenched and unclenched.

"I'd like to get into that," he muttered. "I guess I'm not too old."

Abruptly he turned to the first officer.

"Lower a boat," he said. "I'm going aboard the submarine."

The first officer protested.

"But the passengers—" he began.

"The passengers be hanged," said the captain of the Ventura. "Besides, we're safer here under the nose of this destroyer than we would be prowling off by ourselves."

The first officer protested no longer. A boat was lowered and Captain Griswold and half a dozen sailors climbed in and put off for the submarine, where they arrived just in time to overhear Jack say that if the Germans in the submarine didn't surrender they would go after them. Captain Griswold laid a hand on Jack's shoulder.

"You're some scrapper, youngster," he said.

Jack was thus made aware for the first time that the Ventura had not rushed for her home port.

"I thought you'd gone, Captain," he said.

"I was on my way," said the captain of the Ventura, "until I saw you fighting these murderers single-handed. I came back to see if I could help."

"Thanks," Jack laughed, "but I guess there are enough of us to attend to them without you, Captain."

"I'm not sure about that," declared Captain Griswold. "I just heard you say you were going below after those fellows?"

"Well?" questioned Jack.

"Pretty risky," responded Captain Griswold, shaking his head. "How do you figure to get 'em?"

"Rush 'em," said Jack briefly.

Again the captain of the Ventura shook his head doubtfully.

"Too risky altogether," he declared. "The first one of you that shows his head down there will be potted, sure as fate."

"But we've got to do it, Captain," said Jack. "How else is it to be done?"

"Well," said Captain Griswold, removing his cap and scratching his head, "I guess I can suggest a way."

"I'm open to conviction, Captain," said Jack.

"Aboard my ship," went on Captain Griswold, "I have a supply of a certain sort of gas which, if used properly, will do in minutes what it may take you hours to accomplish."

"By George!" said Frank. "Kill 'em all at once, eh?"

"Well, no, it won't do that," replied Captain Griswold, "but it'll put 'em to sleep long enough for you fellows to go down and tie 'em up."

"Bring on the gas, Captain," said Jack quietly.

Captain Griswold hustled back to his boat with the agility of a small school boy.

"Back to the ship," he roared to the sailors who rowed him.

He mounted the ladder swiftly and summoned his first officer.

"Helgoson," he said, "those Britishers have gone and almost captured that submarine. It's up to us to help 'em complete the job."

"How, sir?" asked the first officer.

"Do you know where that gas tank is below?"

"Yes, sir."

"Fetch it here. It's small enough so you can carry it. Also get the hose and the pump."

"Yes, sir."

The first officer hurried away. He was back in a few moments with the necessary articles, which Captain Griswold took charge of himself.

"Helgoson," said Captain Griswold, "if you were a younger man I would invite you to take a hand in this party yourself. As it is, you'll have to stick behind with the passengers."

"But I'm younger than you by almost twenty years, sir," protested the first officer.

"Oh, no you're not," laughed the commander of the Ventura, "you just think you are. I've grown twenty years younger this day."

He summoned a pair of sailors, whom he loaded down with the gas, hose and pump with instructions to place them carefully in the small boat.

"And now for the submarine," he confided to his first officer.

On deck, half a dozen passengers approached the captain with inquiries as to what was going on.

"Why," he said with a grin, "we're just going to capture a submarine, that's all. Stick close to the side of the ship and you'll see how it's done. A lesson like this may come in handy some day."

The passengers protested.

"But the danger—" one began.

"Danger be hanged," said the captain. "There is no danger. While there was danger we were scuttling for the safety of land and now we come back when it's all over. You should all be glad of this opportunity to render your country a service. What sort of citizens are you, anyhow?"

Without further words he climbed down to the launch and was hustled back to the submarine, where Jack and the others were awaiting him eagerly.

"Well," said Captain Griswold, motioning to the articles that the sailors laid on the deck, "here's the stuff. Get busy."

"How do you work it, Captain?" asked Jack.

"Don't you know?" demanded Captain Griswold. "Well, I'll tell you what. You just put me in command here for fifteen minutes and I'll do the job for you."

"All right, sir," said Jack. "Your commands shall be obeyed."

Captain Griswold turned to the nearest sailor.

"Take that hose and attach it to the nozzle on the tank," he directed. The sailor did so.

"Now the pump," said the captain, "you will find a place for it on the other side of the tank."

This was adjusted to the captain's satisfaction.

"Now," said the captain, "all you have to do is to stick this nozzle down the conning tower, turn it so as to give the gas full play and pump. Of course the gas would carry without the pump, but you save time this way."

"One moment, Captain," said Jack. "How about ourselves? Won't the gas affect us as well as the Germans?"

Captain Griswold clapped a hand to his side.

"Now what do you think of that?" he demanded. "I must be getting old before my time. Here, Lands," he called one of his own men, who approached. "Go and tell Helgoson I want two dozen of those gas masks in the store room; and hustle."

The sailor hurried away. He was back within fifteen minutes, and Captain Griswold distributed the gas masks. Then he took the nozzle of the hose, poked it down the conning tower and looked around.

"Everybody ready?" he asked.

Jack also glanced around. Every man on the deck of the submarine wore a gas mask.

"All right, sir," said Jack.

"Then you turn that screw there when I give the word. All right? Then shoot!"

There was a hissing sound as Jack turned on the gas.

For perhaps ten minutes Captain Griswold moved the hose to and fro. Then he pulled it forth and motioned Jack to turn the screw again. This the lad did. Captain Griswold then motioned the others to follow him, and led the way below.

At the foot of the conning tower they stumbled across several figures, overcome by the fumes. These were quickly bound and passed up on deck to the men who remained behind.

The search of the submarine took perhaps half an hour. Every nook and cranny was explored. The gas had done its work well. Apparently it had poured in so rapidly that the crew had had no time to open the portholes, for they were all closed. Captain Griswold opened them now.

Then he led the way on deck, and closing the conning tower, removed his gas mask. The others followed his example.

"Simple, wasn't it?" said the captain of the Ventura to Jack, grinning like a boy. "Lucky I happened to come back."

"It is indeed," said Jack. "But won't this gas affect us, Captain?"

"Not out here," was the reply. "It's not strong enough. You can barely smell it now. Now what are you going to do with the submarine?"

Jack considered a moment.

"I'll tell you Captain," he said, "it strikes me that this submarine is really the prize of the Ventura. At all events, I cannot be bothered with it, for there is still patrol work to do in these waters. Can't you tow her into port?"

"Can't I?" shouted Captain Griswold. "You bet I can. You give the word and I'll tie her on behind right now."

"All right, Captain," said Jack. "She's yours."

Captain Griswold almost danced a jig there on the deck of the German submarine.

"Won't New York sit up and take notice when old Captain Griswold comes into port towing a submarine?" he chortled. "Well, I guess. Here, Lands, go back to the ship and throw me a line. Then come back and help make it fast."

This was accomplished with astonishing rapidity and amid the cheering of the crew and passengers of the Ventura and the wild hurrahs of the British tars of the Essex.

"Well, she's all fixed," said Captain Griswold, "and to tell you the truth I'm rather sorry. Of course I'm old and all that, but just the same I'd like to go with you fellows."

"You're doing your share, Captain," said Jack seriously. "All of us can't do the fighting, you know. But there's work just as important, and you are doing your part. But we must be moving now. We've wasted time enough."

"So we have," declared Captain Griswold. "Shall you leave us here, sir?"

"No," said Jack, "we'll follow and see you safely in harbor."

"Very well. Then I shall return to the Ventura."

"And I to the Essex, Captain. Good-bye and good luck to you."

Captain Griswold shook hands heartily with Jack, and then insisted on shaking hands as well with Frank, and every officer and member of the British crew aboard the submarine. Then he put off for his ship.

Jack and the others returned to the Essex. When the lad reached the bridge, the Ventura was already moving, the submarine trailing behind.

"A fine man, Captain Griswold," said Frank.

"Right," Jack agreed. "And the U-87 is his so far as I'm concerned. He might hang it on his parlor wall for a souvenir."

"Or wear it as a watch charm," added Frank with a grin.

## CHAPTER XVIII

## ASHORE

For two days the Essex had been cruising up and down the coast on patrol duty, looking for submarines. Several times the destroyer had been ordered farther out to sea to form an escort for an incoming steamer, but after her encounter with the U-87 she had sighted no more of the enemy.

Following the report of two vessels sunk off the coast on May 10, the day on which the presence of German raiders off the coast was first reported, the number of sinkings increased the following day, and the next. After that they fell off, however, and upon the fifth day only one ship—a small schooner—was sent to the bottom off the coast of Delaware.

The prisoners taken from the U-87 were stowed safely away below-decks on the Essex, after which Jack got in touch with Admiral Sellings, on the Dakota, by wireless. He reported the capture of the submarine and the fact that it was being towed into port by the Ventura. Admiral Sellings ordered Jack to continue his patrol of the coast until further notice.

Nevertheless, the Essex escorted the Ventura almost to port, before putting about and resuming her patrol duty.

All the remainder of that day and the two days that followed Jack kept his ship moving up and down the coast, but he caught no sight of an enemy vessel, nor were any of the sinkings reported in that time close enough to be considered within his territory.

On the fourth day came a message from Admiral Sellings.

"German submarine reported twenty miles north of Cape Charles," read the message. "Investigate."

Jack acknowledged receipt of the order and addressed Frank, who stood beside him on the bridge.

"Something definite to act on at last," he said, and read the admiral's message aloud, adding: "Shape your course accordingly, Mr. Chadwick."

Frank gave the necessary directions. The big ship came about and headed south again.

It was well along in the afternoon when the Essex reached the approximate point designated by Admiral Sellings. Jack ran the destroyer as close in-shore as he dared, and for several hours cruised about in the neighborhood. But he saw nothing to indicate the presence of a submarine.

"If there's a U-Boat here, it's keeping pretty well under cover," said Frank.

"So it is," replied Jack. "I don't know where the admiral got his information, but I've got my doubts of its authenticity."

Frank's eyes were caught at that moment by the sight of a small row boat putting off from the shore. He watched it idly for a moment, and then noted that it was headed directly for the Essex.

"Hello," he said, "here comes some one to visit us."

Directly the little boat scraped alongside the now stationary destroyer and the figure in the boat indicated that he wanted to come aboard.

"Don't know what he wants," muttered Jack, "but it'll be just as well to have him up and find out."

A few moments later the occupant stood before Jack and his officers on the bridge.

"My name," he said, "is Charles Cutlip, and I live back there." He waved a hand shoreward. "I suppose you are hunting for submarines, Captain?"

Jack nodded.

"That's what we're here for," he affirmed.

"I thought so," said young Cutlip—he was a little more than a boy. "Well, Captain, maybe I can help you."

Jack gave an exclamation of astonishment.

"What do you mean?" he asked.

"I don't know exactly," replied the boy. "Yesterday afternoon, while I was in the house alone, three strange men appeared at the door. They wore the costume of an ordinary seafaring man, but when they asked me for food they had a strange manner of speech. They weren't Americans, I'm sure of that."

"And you think they were from a submarine, eh?" asked Jack.

"I'm sure of it, Captain. There were no other ships near, and they could not have come overland, for it is a long ways to the nearest village and they had neither horses nor automobile."

"And what did you say to them?" asked Frank.

"I gave them what food there was in the house, but they said it wasn't enough. About this time my father came in unexpectedly. The strangers drew revolvers and covered him. They told him they would be back to-night and that they required him to have a certain amount of food on hand. They threatened to kill him if he gave the alarm—and they threatened to kill me too."

"By George!" exclaimed Frank. "It looks as though we had come to the right spot, Jack."

"It certainly does," agreed Jack. "Now tell us the rest of your tale, son."

"That's about all," said the boy. "They devoured what food I gave them and then disappeared."

"And your father sent you for help, I suppose," added Frank.

"No," said the boy. "I came of my own accord. My father is badly frightened. He has gone to find the food for the strangers. I slipped away and ran toward the sea. Then I saw your ship, sir, and I hurried to tell you."

"You have done well," said Jack, laying a hand on the lad's shoulder. "And now you will be willing to help us further, will you not?"

"Of course I shall, sir."

"Very good. Now you look around the ship to your heart's content, while I hold a conference with my officers."

"Very well, sir."

The boy walked away. Jack held a consultation with his officers on the bridge.

"If the boy is telling the truth," he said, "and I have no doubt of it, we are in luck. It may be that we can capture this German crew ashore and then take possession of the submarine."

"But, sir," protested Lieutenant Hetherton, "if the submarine were to come to the surface now and catch sight of the Essex it would never come back again."

"I had thought of that," replied Jack, "and I have a plan that will offset it. You see that projecting reef there?" and Jack pointed to the north. The others signified that they did. "Well," Jack continued, "back of that is as cosy a little harbor as you would care to see. I noticed it as we came by. We'll take the Essex there, and she will be hidden well enough."

"Unless the submarine should chance to come to the surface there," was Frank's objection.

"We'll have to leave something to chance," declared Jack.

"In which event your plan is as good as any I can conceive," said Frank. "But after we get the Essex there, then what?"

"Why," said Jack, "I'll take a party of half a hundred men or so and surround the house of this Cutlip boy. When the Germans arrive we'll nab 'em. After that we can find the submarine."

"Hasn't it struck you, sir," Frank asked of Jack, "that maybe the men who accosted this boy and his father were merely bluffing? That they may not return to-night?"

"It has," Jack replied, "but at the same time there is a chance that they will. Therefore, in lieu of any other clue as to the whereabouts of the submarine, I deem it well to act on what information, we have."

"It won't hurt anything, that's sure, sir," was Lieutenant Hetherton's comment.

In this the other officers agreed.

"Very well then," said Jack. "It shall be as I suggested. Mr. Chadwick, will you shape your course for the point I have mentioned."

"But the boy, sir?" said Frank. "Shall we not put him over the side first?"

"No; we'll take him with us," Jack decided.

As the destroyer began to forge ahead, the Cutlip boy grew alarmed and hurried to Jack's side.

"You are not taking me away, are you, sir?" he asked fearfully.

"No," replied Jack, and outlined the situation as fully as he deemed wise.

Young Cutlip was plainly eager to help in the capture of the German submarine crew.

"And you feel sure they will come back to-night?" Jack questioned.

"Yes, sir. They must be very hungry. If you could have seen those three men devour what little food I gave them! They seemed to be half starved."

"Strange, too," Jack muttered, "considering the number of ships they have sunk in these waters recently. They should have replenished their stores."

"It may be that this was one of the less fortunate submarines," said Frank. "The sinkings may have been done by other U-Boats."

"That's true, too," said Jack. "I hadn't thought of that. I guess that must be the answer."

Less than an hour later, the Essex passed behind the shelter of the reef Jack had mentioned. There Jack ordered her stopped, and anchor dropped.

"We should be out of sight here," he said, "unless, as you suggested, Frank, the enemy should come to the surface at this point. And we'll have to trust to luck that they don't."

"And now what, sir?" asked Frank.

"I'll let you select a hundred men of the crew for shore duty," said Jack.

This task did not take long, and Frank had picked and armed his men within half an hour.

"Now," said Jack, "I'm going to put you in command of the party, Frank. Lieutenant Hetherton shall go along as your immediate subordinate. Two officers are enough. The rest of us will wait here. But if you have not returned soon after daylight, we'll start a search for you."

"I can see no reason why we should be longer," said Frank. "We'll do the best we can."

"Then I would suggest that you go ashore at once," said Jack. "You must reach the Cutlip home while it is yet daylight in order to lay your plans."

"Right, sir," said Frank, saluting. "We shall go ashore at once."

They put off over the side in small boats and rowed toward the shore, where they landed less than an hour after the Essex dropped anchor. Jack waved a hand to his chum from the bridge.

"Good luck!" he called.

Frank waved back at him, then addressed his men.

"By fours! Forward march!" he commanded.

The party, with young Cutlip in their midst, moved inland.

CHAPTER XIX

IN THE NIGHT

It was not a long march to the Cutlip home, and the Essex party reached there some time before nightfall. Young Cutlip now whispered a word of caution to Frank.

"My father will not like this," he said. "He is naturally a cautious man. If he thinks I have given the alarm—am responsible for your being here—it will go hard with me."

"Then he must not know it," said Frank decidedly. "Do you think he will be home now?"

"Yes, sir; most likely."

Frank considered.

"Then I'll call a halt here," he said. "You can return home and we will come later. In that way he will not know that you gave the alarm. But by the way, when he sees us is he not likely to try and warn the enemy?"

"He might, sir. He is terribly afraid of submarines and men who control them. He appears to think they are something supernatural. He believes the crews of the submarines can whip anyone, sir. That is why he is likely to tarry and give an alarm."

"In that case," said Frank, "we'll have to tie him up until the game is over."

"He's my father, sir, and I don't want you to hurt him," said young Cutlip, "but that would be the best way, sir."

"Very well," said Frank. "You run ahead, now; we'll wait here for an hour."

He called a halt. Young Cutlip ran on ahead. Frank explained the reason for the halt to Lieutenant Hetherton, who agreed that the lad had acted wisely.

"No use getting the boy in trouble if we can help, it, sir," he said.

An hour later Frank ordered the march resumed. Young Cutlip had given necessary directions and the party from the Essex reached the Cutlip home without trouble. As they drew near, a man came to the door of the little cabin that nestled in among a group of trees. Beside him, Frank made out the figure of the boy who had given notice of the visit of some of the submarine crew.

Frank motioned his men to halt some distance away, called Lieutenant Hetherton to follow him, and approached the cabin.

"How do you do, sir?" he asked civilly of the big man in the doorway.

"What do you want here?" was the growling response.

"We're from a British destroyer out there," said Frank, waving a hand in the general direction of the Atlantic, "and we are hunting for submarines that have sunk a dozen or more ships off the coast."

"You don't expect to find them here on land, do you?" demanded Cutlip.

"Not exactly," said Frank. "But I have reason to believe that the crew of one of the vessels has come ashore. Have you seen anything of them, sir?"

"I have not," replied Cutlip firmly.

"No one resembling a German, even?" persisted Frank.

"No."

"You are quite sure?"

"Quite sure."

"Think again, my man," said Frank.

"Look here," said Cutlip, "do you mean to insinuate that I'm lying?"

"I don't insinuate anything. I know you are lying. Hold up there!"

For Cutlip had taken a threatening step forward.

"A party of three German sailors from a submarine nearby were seen to come this way," Frank went on. "You must have seen them. Now, if you are not trying to shield them, tell me where they are."

"I don't know. I haven't seen them."

"Call a couple of men, Lieutenant," said Frank to Hetherton.

Hetherton raised a hand, and two sailors came forward.

"Once more," said Frank to Cutlip, "will you tell me what you know of those men?"

"I tell you I don't know anything," answered Cutlip doggedly.

"Tie him up, men," said Frank briefly.

The sailors sprang forward and laid rough hands on Cutlip. The latter protested vigorously with his mouth, but he offered only feeble resistance.

"Now," said Frank to Hetherton, "we can't leave him around here for if the Germans saw him they might take alarm. We'll have to have him sent back to the ship. I guess those two men are big enough to get him there."

"Plenty big enough, sir," said one of them with a grin.

"Good. Take him back, then, and come back when you have turned him over to Captain Templeton. Tell the captain to hold him until we return."

The man touched his cap.

"Aye, aye, sir," he said. Then to Cutlip in a rough voice: "March, now."

The three disappeared, Cutlip grumbling to himself and the sailors grinning.

Frank turned to young Cutlip, who had watched these proceedings with some disfavor.

"Now, my boy," he said, "we can get ready for business."

"They won't hurt him, will they?" asked the boy, pointing after his father.

"They will not," said Frank. "Only keep him safe until the trouble is over."

"All right. Then, I'll help you the best I can, sir."

"That's the way to talk, my boy. Now let me look around a bit."

Lieutenant Hetherton and young Cutlip accompanied Frank on his tour of inspection. The lad found that the cabin was cuddled securely in a miniature forest, or rather at one end of it. On both sides and in the rear were a profusion of dense trees. Only the approach from the front was in the clear.

"It's all right," Frank said. I'll throw my men around the house from three sides, and when the Germans have gone in we can surround it completely. If they come after dark, there is little doubt they will approach from the front."

"And what shall I do, sir?" asked young Cutlip.

Frank turned the matter over in his mind.

"I am afraid I shall have to ask you to play rather a dangerous part," he said at last. "You must be inside to receive them. If there were no one there they might take alarm and run. Now, we'll go inside and see if your father has complied with the enemy's demand."

The three entered the cabin. Inside, Frank made out several big sacks scattered about the floor. "Potatoes," he said, and looked further. There he also found an extraordinary amount of salt meats and a bountiful supply of vegetables.

"Looks like your good father had been very busy," he said to young Cutlip with a smile. "That's what the Germans will have the whole world doing for them if we don't lick 'em."

"You're right there, sir," agreed Lieutenant Hetherton.

"Well," said Frank, "we'll leave these things as they are. It will help divert suspicion from young Cutlip here when the Germans find his father is not on hand. But I guess there is nothing more we can do now. Come, we'll go outside."

Frank now saw to the disposition of his men. These, as he had decided, he stationed on three sides of the cabin. He himself took command of the men on the left, Lieutenant Hetherton commanding the right wing and a sailor named Hennessy the left. A short time later the sailors who had conducted Cutlip the elder to the Essex returned and took their places.

"Did he go along peaceably?" asked Frank of one of the newcomers.

"Well, he kicked once or twice," replied the man, "but he went along all the same, sir."

Frank grinned.

"Just so long as you got him there," he said.

"Oh, he's there, all right," grinned the sailor, "but when I left he was threatening to have the whole American navy down on us and hoping that these German submarines shoot us to little pieces."

"I think we'll do most of the shooting, if there is any to be done," said Frank dryly.

There was silence in the ranks after this, for it was now growing dark and it was possible that the Germans might appear at any moment. Every man strained his eyes as he peered through the trees.

Inside the cabin a faint light glowed. Young Cutlip was in there, playing a braver part than could his father, doing his best for his country as enemies threatened her existence. Frank smiled to himself.

"A nervy kid," he muttered; "yet, I wish I didn't have to use him. I shall take especial care that no harm comes to him."

He grew silent.

In the distance came the sound of tramping feet—many of them. Gradually they drew nearer and directly Frank could hear voices. Heavy, guttural voices they were and the tongue they spoke was German.

Up to that moment Frank had not been at all sure in his own mind that the Germans would return to the cabin, as they had told the Cutlips. Nevertheless, here they were, and the lad's heart leaped high.

"They must be pretty close to starvation to take such chances," the lad muttered to himself. "Wonder why they don't try a raid on one of the nearby towns? Guess they don't want to stir up any more trouble than possible, though. Well, we'll get 'em."

Frank peered from his hiding place. The Germans were in sight now, and approaching the house four abreast.

"Four, eight, twelve, sixteen, twenty-four," Frank counted.

"That's not so many. We can grab them easy enough."

But a moment later additional footsteps were heard. Again Frank counted moving figures to himself.

"Twenty more," he muttered. "Where on earth did they all come from? By George! They certainly are taking a long chance marching around like this. Well, the more we can get the better."

At the door of the cabin the Germans halted. Three of their number stepped forward and went inside. This was not at all in line with Frank's plans, and he realized now that the situation of young Cutlip, inside, was dangerous in the extreme. Something must be done to protect him.

As the Germans went inside the house, the others, meanwhile, standing guard, Frank gave the signal agreed upon, a soft whistle, like the call of a bird of the night. The British began to move from their hiding places and to draw closer to the Germans, standing there in the open.

"Well," Frank muttered to himself at last, "I guess the sooner we get busy the better."

He sprang to his feet and leaped forward.

## CHAPTER XX

## THE BATTLE

Meanwhile, inside the cabin young Cutlip was facing the Germans cooly enough. He rose to his feet as the door opened and the first German stuck his head inside. The latter surveyed the interior rapidly, and seeing a single figure there, advanced quickly, gun in hand.

"Oho! It's the boy," he said in clumsy English. "And where is your father?"

"I don't know," answered the boy. "He went away."

"But did he get the food?"

Cutlip motioned to the sacks of provisions on the floor.

"Good!" said the German, rubbing his hands.

He returned his revolver to his belt and motioned his two companions to enter. They closed the door behind them.

"You have told no one of our presence here?" asked the first German, as he stooped over to examine the sacks.

"No."

"How about your father?"

"He has told no one, either."

"It is well. For if you had, we would kill you now."

Young Cutlip said nothing, but he knew by the hard look in the man's eyes that he told the truth. In spite of the fact that the boy knew he was in grave peril, he was perfectly cool.

He sat down again as the Germans passed from sack to sack, examining the contents. At last the first man stood up and faced the boy.

"Your father, by chance, didn't say anything about pay for this food, did he?" he asked.

"No," returned Cutlip.

The German grinned.

"Guess he knew it wouldn't do much good," he said. "Well, men, let's roll this stuff outside."

Again the men bent over the sacks.

At that moment there came a shot from without, followed by a volley. On the instant young Cutlip leaped to his feet, rushed to the door, threw it open and dashed outside.

There he was right in the midst of the Germans. But the latter were too busy and too surprised to pay any attention to him at that moment. They had wheeled at the first volley from the woods, and had turned their own weapons against the trees on three sides of the cabin.

Two or three of their number had gone down at the first fire, and they were almost demoralized, so sudden and unexpected was the attack. Consequently, young Cutlip had time almost to get clear of the enemy. In fact, by quick dodging, he did get beyond them.

Out the door now rushed the three Germans in the cabin, apparently in command of the men without. One issued harsh orders, and the Germans dropped to the ground, thus making much smaller targets.

Frank, as he sprang forward from among the trees, saw young Cutlip throw open the door and dash out. Frank ran toward him despite the fact that he was charging the enemy almost single-handed. But he knew that the boy was in danger through no fault of the lad's own, and that he must be protected.

"Here, Cutlip!" he called.

The boy ran toward him.

Frank, a revolver in each hand, stopped and awaited the lad's approach.

Two Germans raised their rifles to shoot Cutlip down. Frank's eye caught the glint of the steel in the darkness. His revolvers spoke sharply twice, and Cutlip came on unharmed.

A bullet sang past Frank's right ear, another grazed his left. More bullets began to sing by him. Cutlip stumbled forward, and sheathing one revolver, Frank caught him by the hand.

"Run!" he cried.

Cutlip needed no further urging. Together he and Frank sped for the shelter of the woods, which they reached safely and threw themselves on the ground as a rain of bullets passed overhead.

"Close shave, son," said Frank.

Young Cutlip was trembling, but he was not afraid.

"Give me a gun," he cried. "I can pick off a few of 'em."

But Frank shook his head.

"You've done your part," he said. "Now you get away from here until we clean these fellows up."

Frank circled among the trees until he came into the midst of his own men again. These were still peppering away at the enemy from among the trees and the Germans, lying on the ground, were returning the fire.

"We're wasting too much time here," Frank told himself.

He looked across to where Lieutenant Hetherton and his men were also blazing away at the foe.

"Forward men!" cried Frank suddenly. "Charge!"

The British tars under Frank's command went forward with a wild yell. Seeing their companions dashing across the open, the forces commanded by Lieutenant Hetherton and the sailor Hennessy also broke from the trees and charged.

The Germans poured several sharp volleys into the attackers, then threw down their arms.

"Kamerad! Kamerad!" came the cry.

"Cease firing!" Frank shouted.

Silence reigned after the noise of the battle.

"Take charge of those men, Mr. Hetherton," said Frank quietly, "but be careful how you approach. I don't trust 'em. I'll keep 'em covered."

Lieutenant Hetherton ordered his men to make prisoners of the Germans.

There came a sudden interruption.

The three Germans who had been in the cabin, as though by a prearranged plan, suddenly dashed back into the little building and flung to the door before they could be stopped.

"Never mind," said Frank, "remove the others, Mr. Hetherton. We'll attend to the men inside later."

From the window of the cabin there came a sharp crack. A bullet zipped by Frank's ear, but the lad did not flinch. He moved his position and saw the German prisoners marched to the rear.

"Now," he said, "we'll have to get those fellows inside. First, however, we'll give them a chance."

He raised his voice in a shout.

"What do you want?" came the response from the cabin.

"You are outnumbered ten to one," said Frank. "Come out and surrender. We don't want to kill you."

"Come and take us," was the sneering response.

"Don't be fools," called Frank. "We're sure to get you."

"Well, I'll get you first," came a sharp cry.

Frank stepped back and none too quickly, for a bullet passed through the space where his head had been a moment before.

"If you must have it, all right," the lad muttered. He turned to his men. "I want ten volunteers to go with me," he said quietly.

Every man stepped forward.

Frank smiled.

"Sorry I can't use you all, men," he said. "But ten will be enough. Gregory, step forward."

A sailor a short distance away did so.

"Now, Gregory," said Frank, "you pick nine more men and bring them here."

This was the work of only a moment, and the men surrounded Frank. For a moment the lad surveyed the cabin. They were now out of the line of fire from the window on that side and consequently safe. It would be possible, Frank knew, to tire the Germans out, but he had no mind for such slow methods. He addressed his men.

"Two of you," he said, "break in the door with your rifle butts. We'll cover you from either side."

Two men stepped forward and the others stationed themselves on either side of the stout door. Frank called to Lieutenant Hetherton.

"Guard all the windows," he shouted. "Don't let them get away."

The door began to tremble under the blows of the two sailors. Directly there was a crash as it fell inward.

Now, although this had been no part of Frank's plans, the minute the door crashed in, the two sailors reversed their rifles and sprang over the threshold.

"Crack! Crack! Crack! Crack! Crack!"

The rifles of the three Germans within and the two British sailors spoke almost as one. One of the tars crumpled up in the doorway, while one of the Germans also threw up his hands and slid to the floor.

With wild shouts of anger, the other sailors surged forward and poured through the door in spite of German bullets, which now flew so fast that accurate aim was impossible.

Frank dashed forward with the others. Down went the second German, leaving but one alive. Frank found himself face to face with the latter.

"Stand back, men," he called.

The sailors obeyed.

In one hand the German gripped a revolver, but Frank held this arm with his left hand and straightened it high above the German's head. Thus the German was unable to bring his revolver to bear on the lad.

Nevertheless, his left arm was still free, and he struck Frank a heavy blow in the stomach with his fist. The pain was severe and Frank loosened his hold on the man's revolver arm. With a cry of triumph, the German deliberately lowered his revolver.

Frank, having dropped one of his revolvers, was in a bad way. True, a second was in his belt, but it did not appear that he had time to draw and fire before the German's finger pressed the trigger.

But now came an action on the lad's part that proved his right to be called an expert with the revolver—an action that often had bewildered Jack and aroused his envy.

So quickly that the eye could not follow the movement, Frank dropped his hand to his belt, whipped out his revolver, and without taking aim, fired.

A fraction of a second later there was a second report, as the German, with Frank's bullet already in his shoulder, pressed the trigger, almost involuntarily. But ere he fired, Frank had dropped to the floor and the bullet passed harmlessly overhead.

Frank rose quietly.

"Bind him men," he said simply. "He's not badly hurt. He'll probably live to face the gallows. Where is young Cutlip? Has anyone seen the boy?"

"Here he is, sir," answered the boy himself, and came forward. "And will you release my father now, sir?"

"As soon as we return to the ship," replied Frank. "Come, men."

CHAPTER XXI

THE END OF THE SUBMARINE

Frank now took account of his casualties. Five men had been killed and twenty more or less seriously wounded. As many more nursed slight injuries.

The enemy's casualties, proportionately, had been more severe. Half of the original number were stretched on the ground. Hardly a man of the others but had been wounded.

Frank had his dead made ready for transportation back to the Essex, and litters were improvised for the wounded who were unable to walk. The grounded Germans also were carried—that is, those of them who were so severely hurt they could not walk. Those who could walk were surrounded by the British and marched on ahead.

The return trip was made without incident. The wounded were hurried aboard the ship where their injuries could be attended to. The unwounded prisoners were promptly locked up below with the other captives. Then Frank and Jack, accompanied by young Cutlip, went to Jack's cabin. The third officer held the bridge.

Frank gave an account of the events of the night as briefly as possible. When he had concluded, Cutlip again asked:

"Will you release my father now, sir?"

"Certainly," said Jack. "You have borne yourself right bravely, and we have much to thank you for, as has your country. It is too bad that your father is not of a different stripe."

The boy's face flushed.

"He's a good father in many ways, sir," he said, "but he seems to be scared to death of the Germans, especially of their submarine boats."

"We'll have him up here before we let him go," said Jack. "Mr. Hetherton, pass the word to have; Cutlip brought to my cabin."

Lieutenant Hetherton left the cabin. He returned a few moments later accompanied by two sailors, who walked on either side of the older Cutlip. The man was still bound.

"Remove his bonds," Jack instructed.

Cutlip's hands were released, and he rubbed them together as he eyed the group in the cabin. His eyes rested on his son.

"So!" he exclaimed, "I had an idea you were at the bottom of this."

"But, father—" began the boy.

"I'll attend to you later," said the father, "not that I'll have need to, probably, for the Germans will attend to both of us. What ails you, anyhow? Don't you know that the Germans eventually will be masters of the world? If we stand in with them, it may help."

"The Germans will never be masters of the world," said Jack. "You are laboring under a delusion, Cutlip. Your son is a brave boy. Not only did he warn us of the presence of a German submarine off the coast, but he rendered such other assistance that the entire crew has been either killed or captured."

Cutlip showed his surprise.

"You can't mean it!" he exclaimed. "Why, how could you overcome them. They are supermen. Ever since the war started I have been reading about them. They are wonderful fighters—marvelous."

"Your trouble, Cutlip," said Frank, "is that you have read too much about them. I know that the country has been flooded with German propaganda, but I'd no idea it had affected anyone like that."

"But—" Cutlip began.

Jack silenced him with a gesture.

"You'll have to change all your ideas now, Cutlip," he said. "You see that the German is not a superman. We have beaten them. Besides, your country is at war with Germany. Only a traitor, or a coward, would refuse to help his country."

Cutlip seemed a bit startled.

"I guess that's true," he said at last. "Yes, I guess you're right."

"You and your son had better remain aboard until morning," Jack continued. "We'll put you both ashore then."

"Jack," said Frank at this point, "don't you think we should make an effort to destroy the submarine before we go?"

"By George! We certainly should," declared Jack. "That had slipped my mind for the moment. We'll have one of the captured officers up and see if he will reveal its hiding place."

One of the Germans—a petty officer—entered the cabin a moment later in response to Jack's summons. Jack explained briefly what he wanted.

"Tell you? Of course I won't tell you," said the young officer. "Why should I? Do you think I am a traitor to my country, or a coward?"

Jack shrugged.

"I was just offering the opportunity," he said.

The officer was removed and one of the men brought in. Jack quizzed him with no better results. One after another the unwounded men were questioned, but none would reveal the location of the submarine.

"Looks like we would have to find it ourselves," said Jack at length. "There is no use questioning any of the others. They won't tell."

Assistance came from an unexpected source.

"Maybe I can help out a bit," said the elder Cutlip quietly.

Jack, Frank and Lieutenant Hetherton looked at him in surprise.

"You mean that you know and will tell?" asked Frank.

"I do. You have made my duty plain to me. No longer am I afraid of the Germans."

"How do you come to know this hiding place?" asked Jack.

"I discovered it to-day by accident. I was standing some distance back on shore when I saw the vessel lying on the water."

"How far from here?"

"Just the other side of the reef."

Jack whistled.

"By Jove! We came awfully close," he said.

"You did indeed," said Cutlip. "But for the reef you must have been discovered. Fortunately, it is very high."

"I suppose the U-Boat is on the surface at this moment," Frank interjected.

"Most likely," Hetherton agreed. "A small crew has probably been left on board, and they more than likely are awaiting the return of their comrades."

"Strange they didn't hear the firing," said Frank.

"Not at all," said Jack. "I heard none of it here."

"The wind was blowing the wrong way," Hetherton explained.

"That must be the answer," Frank admitted. "Well, Jack, what do you say? Shall we make an effort to get the boat to-night?" Jack hesitated.

"We may as well," he said at last. "Of course it will have to be taken from the land, for we can't work the destroyer around the reef in the darkness. Even if we got around safely, we should be discovered."

"Right," said Frank. "Then let's be moving. I take it, however, we will need boats to reach the submarine."

"Our prisoners probably have left all the boats we need," Jack returned.

"That's so," said Frank. "Funny I didn't think of that. Will you be our guide, Cutlip?"

"Glad to be," was the reply. "I want to redeem myself in some way."

"Let's be moving, then," said Frank, starting for the door.

"Hold on," said Jack "We've got to take a force with us, you know. Mr. Hetherton, I'm going to leave you in command of the ship this time. I shall command the shore party."

Lieutenant Hetherton's face fell, but all he said was:

"Very well, sir."

"In the meantime," said Jack, "pick fifty men and set them ashore. We'll be there directly."

Lieutenant Hetherton saluted and left the cabin.

Half an hour later Jack led his men around the reef. There, a scant hundred yards from shore, lay the submarine. The little party moved silently to the edge of the water, and as silently embarked in the half a dozen small boats they found there.

"Push off!" Jack commanded in a whisper.

Now young Cutlip had been left behind, but the father had elected to go with the men in the boats. So earnest was his plea that Jack did not have the heart to refuse him.

A dim light showed on the bow of the submarine as the little flotilla approached; and then so suddenly that the night appeared to be lighted up by magic, a flare of white made the boats approaching the submarine as plain as day.

The submarine's searchlight had been turned on them.

"Down men," cried Jack.

The men, or those of them who were not needed at the oars, dropped to the bottom of the boats. But the distance was so close that those on board were able to make out the fact that the boats approaching were not filled with their own men.

"Americans!" was the cry that carried across the water. "Man the forward gun there!"

"Fire, men!" cried Jack in a loud voice. "Sweep the deck with your rifles. Don't let 'em bring that gun to bear."

There was a crash of rifles as Jack's command was obeyed. Nevertheless the Germans succeeded in training their rapid-firer, and it crashed out a moment later. A veritable hail of bullets flew over Jack's men.

At a quick command from the lads, the boats drew farther apart, thus making the task of the enemy more difficult. Then they closed in on the submarine from both sides.

Harsh German cries and imprecations were wafted to the ears of the British as the boats drew closer.

"Submerge!" shouted a voice.

"Quick, or we shall be too late," Jack roared.

The men at the oars exerted themselves to further efforts. Then Jack caught another cry from the submarine.

"We can't submerge. The tanks are still broken."

"Good!" said Jack to himself. "Now I see what the trouble is. Faster," he cried to his men.

"Quick," came a voice from the submarine, "we cannot let the ship fall into the hands of the accursed Yankees. The fuse, man."

Jack understood this well enough. He raised his voice in a shout:

"Cease rowing!"

Frank's voice repeated the command and the little flotilla advanced no more.

"Put about and make for shore," shouted Jack. "Quick."

The order was obeyed without question, and it was well that it was. Hardly had the boats reached the shore when there was a terrific explosion, and the water kicked up an angry geyser.

"And that," said Jack calmly, "is the end of the submarine. They've blown her up—and themselves with her!"

## CHAPTER XXII

## WASHINGTON AGAIN

Early the following morning the Essex slipped from her little harbor and put to sea. Cutlip and his son, who had been put ashore shortly before the departure, stood at the edge of the water and waved farewell. Following the father's conversion, he and his son seemed to be closer than before, and they went away happily together.

Jack descended to the radio room.

"Get the Dakota for me," he instructed the operator.

"Dakota! Dakota!" flashed the wireless.

Ten minutes later the answer came.

"Destroyer Essex," flashed the operator again, following Jack's direction. "Submarine reported to me yesterday destroyed. Crew either killed or captured."

"Fine work, Templeton," was the reply flashed back a few moments later.

"I'm awaiting instructions," Jack flashed.

"Proceed to Newport News," came the answer, "and report in person to Secretary of the Navy."

"O.K." flashed the operator.

Jack went to the bridge, where Frank was on watch.

"Well, old fellow," said Jack, "I guess our present cruise is ended."

"How's that?" asked Frank.

"We're ordered back to Newport News, and I must report to Secretary Daniels."

"And after that, England again, I suppose?"

"I suppose so."

"Too bad," said Frank, "I would like to have had time to go to New York and Boston to see my father. He could have met me at either place."

"You'll see him when the war's over, I guess," said Jack, "and to my mind that will be before long now."

"Think so?" asked Frank. "Why?"

"Well, take for example the submarine raid off the American coast. It looks to me like the dying gasp of a conquered foe. They must be nearing the end of their rope to tackle such a problem."

"And still they have had some success," said Frank.

"True. But not much after all. What is the total tonnage destroyed in comparison with the tonnage still sailing the seas unharmed?"

"There's something in that," Frank agreed. "But I can't say that I'm of your opinion."

"Personally," declared Jack, "I believe that the war will be over before Christmas."

"I hope so. But I can't be as optimistic as you are."

The run to Newport News was made without incident and the Essex dropped anchor close to the spot where she had been stationed before.

She was greeted with wild cheers, for news of her success had preceded her to the little Virginia city. Jack and his officers and men were hailed with acclaim when they went ashore.

"Want to go to Washington with me, Frank?" asked Jack.

"That's a foolish question," was Frank's reply. "Of course I want to go."

"All right. Then we'll catch the ten o'clock train this morning. That will put us in the capital some time before five."

"Suits me," declared Frank.

This program was carried out. Arrived again in the capital of the nation, the lads went straight to the Raleigh hotel, where they got in touch with the British ambassador.

"I've been hearing good reports about you, Captain," said the ambassador's voice over the telephone.

"We were a bit lucky, sir, that is all," replied Jack deprecatingly.

"Nevertheless," said the ambassador, "Secretary Daniels wishes to thank you in person, as does the President. I shall call for you within the hour."

"Very well, sir."

Jack hung up the 'phone.

The ambassador was as good as his word. He arrived less than an hour later and the lads accompanied him to the Navy Department, where they were ushered into the presence of the Secretary of the Navy at once.

Secretary Daniels shook hands with both of the lads.

"You deserve the thanks of the whole nation for your gallant work," he said. "I am instructed to take you to the President."

Jack and Frank flushed with pleasure, but there was nothing either could say. From the Navy Department, the lads were escorted to the White House immediately across the street, where President Wilson was found in his office. The President was reached with little ceremony, and Secretary Daniels himself made the introduction.

"So," said the President, "these are the young officers who commanded the British destroyer Essex, which accounted for two of the enemy's submarines? They look rather young for such important posts." He gazed closely at Frank. "Surely," he said finally, "surely you are an American."

"Yes, sir," said Frank. "Born in Massachusetts, sir."

"Chadwick," mused the President. "Not, by any chance, related to Dr. Chadwick, of Woburn."

"He is my father, sir."

The President seemed surprised.

"But I didn't know my old friend Chadwick had a son of your age," he said.

"Well, he has, sir," replied Frank with a smile.

"But how do you happen to be in the British service?"

Frank explained briefly.

"You have certainly seen excitement," said the President. "I am glad to have seen you. Give my regards to your father when you see him. I am glad to have met you, too, Captain," and the President shook hands with Jack. "I hope to have the pleasure of meeting you both again some day."

The lads understood by this that the interview was ended. They followed Secretary Daniels and the British ambassador back to the former's office, where the latter handed Jack a paper.

"Cable from the British Admiral, I judge," he said.

Jack read the message.

"You are right, sir," he said. "We are ordered to home waters whenever you are through with us, sir."

"I judged as much," said the Secretary, "which is the reason I had Admiral Sellings order you to report to me. You are at liberty to return whenever you please, sir. But first let me thank you for your services in the name of the American people."

"Thank you, sir," said Jack, and saluted stiffly.

The lads now took their leave. The ambassador insisted on their going home with him to dinner.

"But we should get back to our ship at once, sir," Jack demurred.

"Never mind," said the ambassador, "I'll take the responsibility of holding you over an extra day."

So Jack and Frank dined with the ambassador, and took a late train to Richmond, where they changed early in the morning for Newport News. When they boarded the Essex later in the day they found in Jack's cabin the commandant of Fortress Monroe, who, having learned that the Essex would soon depart for home, had come to pay his respects while he yet had time.

"I want to tell you," he said to Jack, "that the Essex has made quite a name for herself among my men."

"I'm glad to hear that, sir," declared Jack.

"The men are only sorry, and naturally," continued the commandant, "that she was not manned by an American crew."

"Naturally, as you say, sir," Jack agreed. "Yet my first officer is an American."

The Commandant glanced at Frank.

"Can that be true?" he asked.

Frank smiled.

"It's true enough, sir," he said. "Yes, I'm a native of the Bay state and am in the British service merely as the result of an accident."

He explained.

"Well," said the Commandant, 'I'm glad of it. I'll have something to tell my officers and men that will make them proud. I hope that the next time either of you find yourselves in these parts you will look me up."

"Thank you, sir. We certainly shall," said Jack.

The Commandant took his departure.

"And now," said Jack, "for England."

First, Jack made a personal tour of inspection of the destroyer. Finding everything ship-shape, the crew was piped to quarters and Jack rang for half speed ahead.

A crowd had gathered at the water's edge and the Essex was speeded on her way by cheering and waving thousands. It was a touching scene, and Jack was very proud.

"A great country," he confided to Frank, as the vessel moved slowly out into the Roads. "A great country. I am glad to have seen it again, and I hope to come back some day."

"Oh, you'll come back," said Frank. "You'll come back when the war's over, to visit me."

"I certainly will," Jack declared.

The fortifications of Fortress Monroe now loomed ahead.

"I suppose the Commandant is somewhere about to wish us Godspeed," Frank remarked.

The lad was right. And he did it in imposing manner.

The boom of a great gun was heard. This was followed by the roar of many more; and the rumble continued as the Essex drew near, was louder as she breasted the fort and continued as the ship passed on. Jack ordered a reply to the salute from the forward guns, and for the space of several minutes, the very sea seemed to tremble.

Then the Essex gathered speed and plowed ahead.

"Quite an ovation," said Frank, as he and Jack descended to the latter's cabin, leaving Lieutenant Hetherton on the bridge.

"It was, indeed. Yes, as I said before, it's a great country. You should be proud to be a native of it."

"I am," said Frank simply.

## CHAPTER XXIII

## BACK IN ENGLAND

Following the return of the Essex to English waters, Jack reported at once to Lord Hastings in Dover.

"I hear great things of you boys," said Lord Hastings. "Great things indeed."

"We were a bit fortunate, sir," Jack admitted.

"It was more than good fortune," declared Lord Hastings. "But it's nothing more than I expected of you both."

They conversed about various matters for some minutes. Then Jack asked:

"And what is in store for us now, sir?"

"You will report to Admiral Beatty," said Lord Hastings. "The Essex will be assigned to duty with the Grand Fleet in the North Sea. Patrol work, mostly. There is little likelihood that the Germans will make another effort, but the sea must be patrolled, nevertheless."

"When do we report, sir?"

"At once. You will weigh anchor in the morning. Admiral Beatty's flagship is somewhere off the coast of Belgium."

"Very well, sir," said Jack, and departed.

The next day the Essex left Dover. Fifty miles out, Jack picked up the flagship by wireless and received his instructions.

Days lengthened into weeks now and weeks into months and the Essex was still patrolling the North Sea with others of the Grand Fleet—composed besides British vessels of an American squadron in command of Vice-Admiral Sims. August passed and September came and still the Germans failed to venture from their fortress of Helgoland and offer battle to the allies.

The work became monotonous. Occasionally, the Essex put back to port for several days to replenish her bunkers and to take on provisions. At such times Jack and Frank usually went ashore for short periods, and the crew, portions at a time, were granted shore leave.

It was upon the last day of September that great news reached the fleet—news that indicated that the war was nearing its end and that now, if ever, the German fleet might venture from its hiding place and risk an engagement.

Bulgaria had broken with Germany and sued for a separate peace.

Several days later came the news that an armistice had been signed and that Bulgaria had ordered all German and Austrian troops to leave her boundaries. King Ferdinand abdicated in favor of his eldest son, Boris, who immediately ordered the demobilization of the Bulgarian armies.

"Turkey will come next, mark my words," declared Frank as he and Jack stood on the bridge, looking off across the broad expanse of the North Sea.

"Most likely," Jack agreed; "and after Turkey, Austria. That will leave Germany to fight the world by herself."

"She'll never attempt that," Frank declared. "The minute she sees her last chance gone, she'll squeal for help, the same as a hog. It's not in a German to take a licking, you know. He begins to show, yellow when the game goes against him."

"Perfectly true," said Jack, with a nod. "Now, it strikes me that Germany, facing the problem of fighting it out alone—for she must see that Bulgaria's action will soon be followed by her other allies—may send out her fleet for a grand blow."

Frank shook his head.

"Not a chance," he said.

"But," said Jack, "it has been the opinion of war critics and experts right along that Germany was saving her fleet for the final effort when all other means had failed."

"I don't care what the experts think," declared Frank, "I don't think the Germans will dare risk an engagement. In the first place, it would be suicidal—she would have everything to lose and nothing to gain. Don't fret. The German naval authorities know just as well as we do what would happen to the German fleet should it issue from Helgoland."

"Maybe you're right," said Jack, "but in the enemy's place, I wouldn't give up without a final effort."

"That's just it," Frank explained. "You wouldn't, and neither would I. Neither, for that matter, would any British or American officer, nor French. But the German is of different caliber. He doesn't fight half as well when he knows the odds are against him. No, I believe that the German fleet will be virtually intact when the war ends."

"Then we'll take it away from them," declared Jack.

"I'm sure I hope so. It would be dangerous to the future peace of the world to allow the Germans to keep their vessels."

"Well," said Jack, "you can talk all you please, but you can't convince me our work is over—not until peace has been declared—or an armistice signed, or something."

"I agree with you there. There will be plenty of work for us right up to the last minute."

As it developed the lads were right.

"It was shortly after midnight when Jack was aroused by the third officer.

"Message from Admiral Beatty, sir," said the third officer, and passed Jack a slip of paper.

Jack read the message, which had been hastily scribbled off by the radio operator.

"German squadron of six vessels reported to have left Helgoland and to be headed for the coast of Scotland," the message read. "Proceed to intercept them at full speed. Other vessels being notified."

Jack sprang into his clothes, meanwhile having Frank summoned from his cabin. Frank dashed into Jack's cabin, clothes in hand.

"What's up?" he demanded.

"Germans headed for the Scottish coast," replied Jack briefly, and dashed out of the door.

Frank followed him a few moments later. Jack was standing on the bridge giving orders hastily.

"Have a look at the engine room, Frank," said Jack, "and tell the engineer to crowd on all possible steam. We'll have need of speed this trip, or I miss my guess."

Frank obeyed.

The Essex, which had been proceeding east by south at a leisurely pace, had come about now and was dashing due north at top speed. Jack himself shaped the course and gave the necessary instructions to the helmsman.

Below in the radio room, the wireless began to clatter. The operator, from time to time, was getting into touch with other vessels of the Grand Fleet ordered north to intercept the German raiders.

First he received a flash from the Lion; then the Brewster replied, and after her, the Tiger, Southampton, Falcon, White Hawk and Peerless. Counting the Essex this made eight ships speeding northward to intercept the enemy.

"I take it," said Jack, "that this is about the last blow the enemy will attempt to deliver. The Germans, knowing they are beaten, are intent now only upon doing what damage they can while there is yet time. This raid, I suppose, they figure will throw a scare into the coast cities, as similar raids did earlier in the war. However, they'll have a surprise this time, for all the coast ports are fortified now. There will be guns there to stand them off until we get there."

"Let's hope we get there in time," muttered Frank. "I'd like one more crack at the enemy. I'm afraid they are going to get off too easily when peace comes."

"We've got to get there in time," declared Jack.

From time to time the radio operator sent reports to Jack giving the positions of other vessels rushing to the defense of the coast ports.

"We'll get there first, at this rate," said Jack. "We're closer than the others."

"But we're no match for the enemy single-handed," declared Frank. "Chances are that the German squadron is composed mostly of battleships."

"True enough," Jack admitted, "but we'll do what damage we can. The Tiger, Lion, White Hawk, Falcon and Peerless are warships, you know. They'll be more than enough for the foe."

"Yes; but we may be at the bottom of the sea by that time."

"Don't worry. We'll hold our own until assistance arrives."

Jack made a rapid calculation.

"If we had any idea of the approximate position of the enemy at this time, we would know better how to go about our work," he said.

"You might call the enemy and find out?" said Frank with a grin.

"Don't be funny, Frank," said Jack severely. "This is no time for levity."

Came a cry from the lookout.

"Battle squadron off the port bow, sir!"

Jack clapped his glass to his eye.

The ships were too far distant and the night was too dark, however, to permit him to ascertain the identity of the approaching vessels.

"May be the enemy, Jack," said Frank.

"Right," Jack agreed.

A shrill whistle rang out on the Essex.

This was the answer to Jack's order to pipe the crew to quarters.

"Clear ship for action!" was Jack's next command.

"If it is the enemy," he confided to Frank, "we'll try and keep him engaged until reinforcements arrive."

"It may not be so hard, after all," Frank said "They may turn and beat a retreat when they find they are discovered."

"Not if there is only one of us," said Jack. "Pass the word to the forward lookout to sing out as soon as he can identify the enemy. I'll flash my light on them. He may be able to make them out."

The huge searchlight of the Essex flashed forth across the water, and played upon the approaching ships.

"Germans!" came the cry from the lookout.

"I thought so," said Jack. "Frank, go to the radio room and find out how close our nearest support is."

Frank was back in a few minutes.

"Lion says to engage," he reported. "Says she'll be with us in less than an hour. Tiger says she will arrive not more than fifteen minutes later. Falcon and Hawk report they are less than an hour and a half away."

"Right," said Jack. "Trouble is those fellows are likely to out-range us, in which event we'll have to retire slowly, trying to draw them after us. In that way reinforcements may arrive sooner. Hello! There she goes!"

The roar of a great gun came across the water.

## CHAPTER XXIV

## THE ENGAGEMENT

"If we retire," said Jack, "we will leave the way open to the coast. At this minute we are in their way."

"But if we try to stick it out here we'll be sunk," said Frank. "And if we retire toward the coast, we'll be moving away from our supports."

"True enough," Jack agreed. "There's only one thing to do. That is to retire as slowly as possible and try to entice all six ships after us. But I'd much rather wade right in."

"Same here. But discretion is the better part of valor, you know."

"Boom!"

Again a gun spoke aboard one of the enemy.

"We're still out of range," said Jack. "Let 'em come a little closer."

As Jack could now see, all six ships had altered their course slightly and were heading directly for the Essex.

"You may come about, Mr. Chadwick," said Jack.

Slowly the Essex swung about.

"Train your left guns on the enemy," Jack ordered.

This was done.

"Range finders!"

"Still out of range, sir," was the report.

"All right But let me know the minute we can strike."

"Aye, aye, sir."

"Half speed ahead, Mr. Chadwick."

"Aye, aye, sir."

Frank signalled the engine room.

"Boom! Boom! Boom!"

Guns spoke simultaneously aboard three of the enemy ships.

"Still beyond range."

It was Lieutenant Hetherton who spoke.

"Trouble is," said Frank, "that they will be within range before we are."

"We'll risk it," said Jack. "It's up to us to keep them busy until the warships arrive."

The next fire from the enemy resulted in a screaming shell to port.

"They've got the range, sir," said Frank.

"Make it two-thirds speed ahead."

The speed of the Essex increased.

But the German vessels were bearing down on her swiftly, and eventually Jack was forced to call for full speed ahead.

But still the German warships gained.

"They've the heels of us, too," muttered Jack. "Well, we'll slow down a bit and trust to luck. We can't do any damage unless we get within range."

The Essex slowed suddenly to half speed.

The German fleet dashed ahead, now in single formation. This was fortunate for the Essex, for it meant that the guns of only one ship could be brought to bear on the British destroyer at one time.

"Range, sir!" cried the range finder at this point.

"Then fire!" shouted Jack to the aft turret battery captain.

The battery spoke sharply, and the men gave a cheer of delight.

The first shell went home. It cleared the bow of the first German vessel apparently by the fraction of an inch and smashed squarely into the bridge. The crash of the shell striking home was followed almost instantly by an explosion. Timber and steel, intermingled with human bodies, flew high in the air. This much those aboard the Essex could see by the flare of the searchlight.

"A good shot, men!" cried Jack. "An excellent shot!"

An excellent shot it was indeed.

Something appeared to have gone wrong with the steering apparatus of the first German ship. She veered slightly to port.

The target thus presented was an excellent one.

"Fire!" cried Jack again.

The aft battery crashed out and once more the British cheered.

Two shells plowed into the crippled German just on the water line.

"A death wound," muttered Frank.

The lad was right.

The German vessel staggered under the force of the impact and seemed to reel backward. Men leaped to the rails and hurled themselves into the sea.

Suddenly there was a loud explosion and the ship seemed to split in two, a blaze of red fire stretching high into the heavens from the middle of the vessel as it did so. Then blackness enveloped it again and the two parts of the ship fell back into the water with a hiss like that of a thousand serpents. The first German ship was gone.

It was first blood to the Essex and the crew cheered again.

But the other five German vessels came on apace. The gun on the forward ship spoke, but the shell went wild.

"If they'll keep that formation, we might get away with the whole bunch of them," said Frank.

"Yes, but they won't," replied Jack.

He was a good prophet.

Even now, the German vessels began to spread out, and within ten minutes had formed a semi-circle. It was possible now for the forward guns on each ship to rake the Essex without interfering with each other's fire.

"Train your guns on the ship farthest to port," Jack instructed.

The order was obeyed. Again came the order for range finders, and the report that the range was O.K.

"Fire!" cried Jack.

Once more fortune was with the crew of the Essex. The range had been absolutely accurate, and the heavy shell from the Essex carried away the superstructure of the German. At the same moment came a cry from the lookout aft:

"Warship coming up astern, sir!"

Quickly Jack looked around.

"The first of our reinforcements," he said quietly.

He gave his attention again to the enemy, who was drawing uncomfortably close.

"Crash!"

Jack whirled sharply.

A shell had struck the Essex just above the water line on the port side.

"Go below and report, Mr. Chadwick!" Jack ordered.

Frank hurried away in response to this command. He sought the engine room.

"What's the damage, chief?" he asked.

"Slight," was the reply. "Shell passed clear through us, but cleared the boilers. Better round up the carpenter, though, sir."

Frank hurried back to the bridge and reported the extent of the damage. Then he sent a midshipman for the ship's carpenter.

"Crash! Bang!"

Another shell had struck the Essex, this time in the aft gun turret.

"Report, Mr. Chadwick," said Jack briefly.

Frank hurried to the turret.

"What's the damage, Captain?" he asked of the chief of the gun crew.

"One gun smashed, sir," was the reply. "Three of the crew killed and five injured."

"Other guns still working?"

"Can't you hear 'em, sir?"

Frank smiled in spite of himself and cast a quick glance around.

In spite of the death that had overtaken their comrades, the surviving gun crews in the turret were working like Trojans. The big guns continued to spit defiance at the enemy.

Now and then a cheer rose on the Essex as a shot went home.

Frank again returned to the bridge to report.

"Boom!"

It was a deeper voice that spoke this time.

The radio operator himself rushed to the bridge.

"Lion firing, sir," he said. "Says she has sighted us and for us to retire. No need of sacrificing ourselves Captain Jacobs says. The enemy can't get away."

At the same moment the lookout aft sang out again.

"Warship coming up astern, sir!"

"The second of our reinforcements," said Jack quietly. "I'll bet these fellows wish they had stayed home."

"I'm betting the same way," declared Frank.

"Well, it's getting too hot here," said Jack. "We'll get back and let the big fellows get in the game."

"Good idea, sir," said Lieutenant Hetherton.

"Full speed ahead!" Jack ordered.

At the sound of the great gun on the British warship Lion, the German admiral in command of the flotilla ordered his ships to slow down. Until that moment he had not been appraised of the fact that the German raid was known to the British fleet. He supposed, upon seeing the Essex, that he had encountered a single vessel which just happened to be in that part of the sea, but when the Lion came into the fight he began to have his doubts.

As yet, however, there was no other vessel in sight, and as the Germans heavily outnumbered the British, the admiral decided to continue the engagement.

"I suppose this fellow happened to hear the firing and came to investigate," muttered the German admiral. "Our raid can hardly have been discovered yet."

Accordingly he gave the word to advance again.

And a moment later he was sorry that he had done so.

Far astern of the Lion, and yet not so far that the German admiral could not have seen her but for the darkness, came two other long gray shapes; and from farther east, and closer, appeared a third.

The German admiral gritted his teeth.

"Confound these English!" he exclaimed. "Can nobody beat them?"

For a moment he debated with himself. He had half a mind to continue the struggle, for the odds were still, with the Germans. Then he changed his mind.

The wireless aboard the German flagship flashed a signal to retire.

But the German admiral had delayed too long for a successful retreat. Other British ships hove into view—seven of them. There was nothing for the German fleet to do but fight it out. The admiral gave the order:

"Advance!"

## CHAPTER XXV

## THE LAST SEA BATTLE

The cannonading became terrific.

Now that assistance arrived, Jack ordered the Essex, which still was the nearest British vessel to the enemy, back into the fray.

"The big fellows will look out for us," he confided to Frank.

The revolving turrets of the Essex were kept on the move and guns crashed as fast as they could be brought to bear. Shells struck on all sides of the destroyer and occasionally one came aboard. But thanks to Jack's maneuvering of the vessel, so far she had not been struck in a vital part.

The main British fleet bore down on the enemy from two sides, and to protect themselves against these new foes, the Germans were forced to turn their attention elsewhere than the Essex. Already big shells from the British warships were striking aboard the enemy. The range had been found almost with the first fire from the approaching war vessels and the Germans were replying as fast as they were able.

The fighting was at such close range now that Jack was able to distinguish the names of the German battleships. In the center, flying the flag of Admiral Krauss, was the Bismarck. On the right of the flagship were the Hamburg and the Potsdam, while on the left the flagship was flanked by the Baden and the Wilhelm II.

The fire of all five German vessels, at order of the admiral, was now directed upon the Lion, which bore down swiftly and was perhaps a quarter of a mile closer to the enemy than any other British craft except the destroyer Essex, commanded by Jack.

The forward guns of the Lion roared angrily and spat fire in the darkness as she bore down on the Germans at full speed. As yet no enemy shell had struck the Lion, but she had put several shells aboard the nearest German battleship—the Baden.

Now that the German fire had been momentarily lifted from the Essex, Jack ordered his ship in closer; and a veritable hail of shells were dropped on the Potsdam. For a moment or so the Germans paid no attention to the destroyer, but the fire from Jack's men became so accurate that the captain of the German ship found it necessary to disregard the admiral's orders and turn his attention to the Essex in self-defense.

The first shell from the Potsdam flew screaming over the bridge of the destroyer, but did no damage. The second was aimed better. It struck the bow of the destroyer on the port side and plowed through. The destroyer quivered through her entire length.

"Go below and report, Mr. Chadwick," Jack commanded.

Upon investigation, Frank learned that the shell had plowed through the forward bulkheads and that the outside compartments were awash. But the inner compartments had not been penetrated. He rounded up the ship's carpenter, who announced that the damage could be repaired in half an hour. There had been no casualties.

Jack accepted Frank's report with a brief nod; then gave his attention again to fighting his ship.

Forward and to the right of the Essex there sounded a terrific explosion, followed by a blinding glare. The Baden, one of the largest of the German warships, sprang into a mighty sheet of flame. A shell from the Lion had penetrated the engine room and exploded her boilers. Came wild cries from aboard the vessel and escaping steam and boiling water poured on the crew and scalded them.

With the searchlights of the British ships playing on her, the Baden reared high out of the water, and as men jumped into the sea for safety, she settled by the head, and sank.

This left only four of the enemy to continue the struggle and opposed to these the British offered eight unwounded vessels. Admiral Krauss gazed in every direction, seeking a possible avenue of escape. And at last he believed he saw it.

To the east—back in the direction from which he had come—the space between the British battleships Peerless and Falcon seemed to offer a chance. The German admiral calculated rapidly. To the eye it appeared that the German ships could pass through that opening before the British could close in.

The wireless aboard the German flagship sputtered excitedly. Instantly the four remaining German ships turned and dashed after the flagship, which was showing the way.

Instantly the commander of every British ship realized the purpose of the enemy. Even the distant Falcon and Peerless seemed to know what was expected of them. Their speed increased and they dashed forward in an effort to intercept the enemy.

It was nip and tuck. The Lion was the first to dash in pursuit, followed by the Tiger and the White Hawk. The Brewster and Southampton, closely followed by the more or less crippled Essex, brought up the rear, each doing its utmost to pass the other in order to get another chance at the enemy.

Slowly the Lion, the Tiger and the White Hawk gained on the enemy; and it became apparent now that the Germans would be unable to get through the space between the Peerless and Falcon without a fight.

Aboard the Bismarck, the German admiral gritted his teeth.

"It will have to be fight now," he muttered, "and the odds are all against me."

The Falcon and the Peerless, from either side and forward of the Germans, now opened with their big guns almost simultaneously. Every available gun aboard the German vessels replied. From astern, the guns of the Lion were pounding the sterns of the fleeing enemy battleships. The Brewster and the Southampton, together with the Tiger and the White Hawk, also were hurling shells after the Germans, although with little effect, for they were trailing too far behind.

Jack urged the Essex forward in the wake of the others. He was far behind and was rapidly being outdistanced by the larger ships, but he determined to see the thing through if possible.

The last German ship in line, struck by a shell from the pursuing Lion, staggered and fell to one side. The Lion darted on, pouring a broadside into the crippled enemy as she passed, then dashed after the vessels ahead.

The Tiger, White Hawk, Brewster and Southampton, also poured broadsides into the Wilhelm II as they passed, but they did not even slacken their pace.

But the Wilhelm II apparently had not received her death blow. Her crew continued to fight the ship heroically, and as the Essex approached she was greeted with a heavy fire from the German.

"The big fellows don't seem to have made a very good job of this," said Jack to Frank. "We'll finish it for them."

The Essex slowed down and turned sharply toward the Wilhelm II. Her guns still in condition to fight burst forth anew. The British showed excellent marksmanship. Shell after shell was poured into the crippled foe. Jack ordered "cease firing."

Taking a megaphone that lay nearby, he put it to his mouth and called:

"Surrender!"

His answer was a shell that came crashing aboard aft from one of the Wilhelm II's big guns. Jack turned quietly to Frank.

"Sink her!" he said.

Frank dashed across the deck to where the crew of the forward gun turret was anxiously awaiting some command. He addressed the captain of the crew.

"See if you can put a shell into her engine room," he said. "Take your time."

The latter did so; and it was several seconds before the big gun spoke, but when it did Frank uttered an exclamation of satisfaction.

The shell had gone true. Watching eyes aboard the Essex saw it plow its way through the side of the Wilhelm II. Then came the explosion and the Wilhelm II seemed to part in the middle. She sank in less than five minutes.

Meanwhile, the Peerless and Falcon had headed off the other three German ships, which, forced to fight, now stood at bay, with every gun pounding. The Lion, Tiger and the other vessels bore down on them rapidly from astern.

For the space of half an hour the view of those aboard the Essex was obscured by the smoke from the big guns, which could not be penetrated even by the bright lights of the searchlights. They could hear the boom of the big guns, the crash of the shells as they struck home and occasional sharp explosions that told of irrepairable damage aboard the enemy vessels, but they could see nothing.

"This will be the last of the enemy," was Frank's comment.

Jack nodded.

"I should think so," he agreed. "If they let one of those fellows get away now they should be court-martialed."

"Don't fret," said Frank, "they won't get away."

They didn't get away.

Firing ceased just as the first streak of light appeared in the eastern sky, and when the smoke of battle cleared away, Jack and Frank saw that the British victory had been complete.

Only two German ships were still above water. These were the Bismarck, flagship of Admiral Krauss, and the Hamburg. The others had all been sunk.

The Hamburg, the lads could see, was slowly sinking by the head. She was being abandoned by her crew, who, in small boats, some even swimming, were hurrying to the side of the Bismarck, where they were lifted aboard.

"Why didn't they sink her, too?" demanded Frank pointing to the German flagship.

"Why?" repeated Jack. "Why should they? Can't you see that white flag flying at the masthead?"

"By George! I hadn't noticed that."

"And there," said Jack, pointing, "goes a prize crew from the Lion to take over the vessel."

A launch loaded with British tars had put off from the Lion and was making toward the German flagship.

Admiral Krauss and his officers and men were soon transferred to the Lion and a British crew was in possession of the Bismarck.

Thus ended the last sea battle of the great war. In all the times that Germany had tested the naval power of Great Britain and her allies, she had found it great—too much for German naval tactics to overcome. And now that the great war was drawing to an end, she did not test it again.

## CHAPTER XXVI

## THE END APPROACHES

With the coming of November, it became apparent to every officer and man in the Grand Fleet—as well as the rest of the world—that the beginning of the end was at hand—that the German war machine was disintegrating and was about to break.

This was strengthened by the announcement on November 2 that the preceding day England, France and Italy had concluded an armistice with Turkey, thus depriving Germany of her second ally. This left only Germany and Austria to continue the struggle, and upon the same day that the armistice with Turkey was announced came word that Austria also had made overtures for peace.

"You can take it from me," said Jack, as the destroyer Essex continued her patrol of the North Sea, "that this war is about to end. I'm willing to bet that Germany will sue for peace within a couple of weeks."

Frank expressed his doubts.

"She's likely to continue the struggle for some time yet," he said.

"But that would be foolish," declared Jack. "She can hope to gain nothing thereby."

"Perhaps not. But if Germany sues for peace now there is likely to be such an internal upheaval in the Empire that the French revolution will look like a house party."

"Maybe you're right, but I stick to my opinion nevertheless."

Events proved that Jack was right.

On the morning of November 5, word reached the Grand Fleet that an armistice had been concluded with Austria the day before.

"As I expected," said Jack. "What did I tell you, Frank?"

"Well, I anticipated that myself," said Frank. "But Germany hasn't asked for peace yet, you know."

"True, but I can tell you something you don't know. I just got word this morning."

"What's that?"

"Why Germany, through Chancellor Ebert, already is in negotiations with President Wilson."

"What?"

"Exactly. President Wilson has replied that he will stick to his original principles of peace, announced some time ago. Germany is requested to announce whether she will accept such terms."

"But it seems to me," said Frank, "that if Germany wants peace she should be made to ask it on the field of battle."

And that is exactly what happened, for when the armistice negotiations were finally begun it was at a conference between Marshal Foch, commander-in-chief of all the allied forces, and a commission of German officers.

It was on November 8, that news of the armistice conference was flashed to the Grand Fleet.

"Armistice commission will meet November 10 at Hirson, France," read the message, flashed to every vessel in the fleet.

All that day and the next, every man in the fleet waited anxiously for further word of the approaching armistice conference. None came. Neither had any word been received on the evening of November 10.

"Must have been a hitch some place," said Frank, as they sat in the latter's cabin that night.

"Not necessarily," replied Jack, "You know these things take time. A matter like this can't be fixed up in an hour, or a day."

"Well," said Frank, "I'd like to know what terms Marshal Foch will impose on the foe."

"They'll be stringent enough, don't you worry," said Jack. "He'll impose terms harsh enough to make sure that Germany doesn't renew the struggle while final peace negotiations are in progress."

"I hope so. But I'll tell you one thing I hope he does."

"What's that?" Jack wanted to know.

"I hope he insists on the surrender of the whole German fleet."

"Whew!" exclaimed Jack. "You don't want much, do you?"

"Well, he should insist on it," declared Frank.

"But he probably won't," returned Jack. "I figure, however that he will insist that a large share of the ships be turned over to the allies, including their most powerful submarines and battleships and cruisers. But you can't expect them to give up the whole business, particularly when the entire High Seas Fleet is practically intact."

"Maybe not; but I'm for taking all we can get."

"So am I," Jack agreed, "all that we can get without danger of causing a hitch in the armistice proceedings."

"Seems to me," said Frank, "that by this time we should have had some word of the proceedings at Hirson to-day."

"It would seem so, that's a fact. However, I guess we will get the information all in good time."

"That's all right. But I'm anxious to know what's going on."

"Well, we won't know to-night; so I am in favor of turning in."

"Guess we may as well."

But early the next morning, an account of the first day's proceedings of the armistice delegates was flashed to the fleet. This, however, did not bring much jubilation, for the announcement simply said that the German delegates had refused the terms offered by Marshal Foch and had returned to their own lines for further instructions.

"Told you so!" exclaimed Frank. "This war is not over yet."

"Don't you believe it," declared Jack. "These Germans may do a little bluffing—I'd probably try the same thing under similar conditions—but you mark my words, they'll accept the terms, all right."

"The conference is to be resumed some time this afternoon," said Frank. "That means that we will hear nothing before morning."

"It depends," said Jack. "If the armistice is signed to-day, we'll probably get the word immediately; but if it stretches out for a day or two, we probably won't"

"I guess that's about the size of it," Frank admitted.

All during the day excitement aboard the Essex, and all other vessels patrolling the North Sea, for that matter, was at fever heat. While every man knew that there was little likelihood of receiving news until long after dark, each one nevertheless lived in hopes.

Nevertheless, patrol work was still being done carefully. It had become an axiom of a British sailor that a German was not to be trusted—that when he appeared the least dangerous, it was time to watch him more carefully. Consequently, in spite of the impending armistice, the vigilance of the British fleet was not relaxed.

Six o'clock came, and seven; and still there had been no word from the scene of the armistice conference. At eight o'clock Frank said:

"I don't know what we are sitting up for. Something must have gone wrong again. If the armistice had been signed we would know something of it by this time."

"Hold your horses," said Jack. "I'm just as anxious as you are, but there is no use getting excited about it."

"Well," said Frank, "if we haven't heard something by nine o'clock, I'm going to turn in."

But at nine o'clock no word had been received.

"I know we shall hear nothing to-night," said Frank, rising, "so I'm going to tumble into my bunk."

"Help yourself," said Jack, looking up from a book he was reading. "I'll wait a little longer."

Frank retired to his own cabin and was soon asleep. At ten o'clock, no word having been received, Jack put down his book and rose.

"Frank may be right," he told himself. "At all events, I may as well turn in. My remaining up won't alter the facts, whatever they are."

He undressed, extinguished the light in his cabin and climbed into bed.

Aboard practically every ship in the fleet, almost the same scenes were enacted that night. Officers and men alike remained up for hours, awaiting possible word that the armistice had been signed. But at midnight no word had been received, and while the big ships moved about their patrol work, the men slept—those of them who had no duties to perform at that hour. Only the officers and members of the crew watch, and the night radio operators, remained awake.

To Jack it seemed that he had just closed his eyes when he was aroused by the sound of the Essex's signal whistle. It screeched and screeched. Jack leaped from his bunk and scrambled into his clothes.

"Something wrong," he muttered. "Wonder why they didn't call me?"

He hurried on deck.

Frank, in his cabin, also had been aroused by the noise. He, too, sprang into his clothes and hurried on deck.

There the first thing that his eyes encountered was a circle of figures, with hands joined, dancing about the bridge and yelling at the top of their voices. Among them was Jack, who, for the moment, seemed to have forgotten the dignity that went with his command. Also, the shrill signal whistle continued to give long, sharp blasts. Frank looked at Jack in pure amazement.

"Must have gone crazy," he muttered.

He hurried to the bridge and standing behind the dancing figures, caught Jack by the coat as he whirled by.

"I say," he demanded. "What's the meaning of this? Have you gone mad?"

Jack stopped and broke away from the circle which danced on without him.

"Almost," said Jack, in answer to Frank's question, "and with good reason."

"What—" began Frank.

"By George! Can't you think?" demanded Jack.

Gradually comprehension dawned on Frank.

"You mean—" he began again.

"Of course, I mean it," shouted Jack. "Why else do you think I'd be dancing around here like a whirling dervish? Come on and join the crowd. The armistice has been signed!"

"Hurrah!" shouted Frank.

A moment later he was circling madly about the bridge with the others.

## CHAPTER XXVII

### PREPARING FOR THE SURRENDER

ALTHOUGH the armistice had now been officially signed and fighting had ceased, under orders from Admiral Beatty, commander of the Grand Fleet, every ship was still stripped for action. While it appeared that everything was open and above-board, the British admiral intended to take no chances. He recalled other German treachery and he was not at all sure in his own mind that the enemy might not attempt some other trick.

Two days after the signing of the armistice, upon instructions from the admiralty, Admiral Beatty got in touch by wireless with the German fleet commander in Helgoland, Admiral Baron von Wimpfen. With the latter Admiral Beatty was to arrange for the surrender for such portions of the German High Seas Fleet as had been decided upon by Marshal Foch and the German armistice commission.

All day the wireless sputtered incessantly aboard the flagship, while other ship commanders within radio distance listened to what was going on. Jack was among these. He relieved his radio operator for the day and took the instrument himself.

"The German fleet," ticked Admiral Beatty's flagship wireless, "will steam forth from Helgoland on November 19 and move due west toward the English coast, where the British fleet will be stationed to await its coming."

"Shall we dismantle our guns?" asked Admiral von Wimpfen.

"Yes."

"And what of the size of our crews?"

"They shall be large enough to handle the vessel. That is all. The crew of each ship shall be reduced to the minimum."

"And how about our submarines?"

"They must be surrendered first."

"But the surrender cannot be completed in one day."

"I am aware of it," replied Admiral Beatty. "As I have instructed you, the first of the German fleet will leave Helgoland on the night of November 19. By that I mean the submarines. They must steam on the surface. The first flotilla to be composed of twenty-seven vessels."

"I understand," returned the German admiral.

"Very well. My ships will be stretched out in a fifty-mile line on either side of your ships as they approach and will fire at the first sign of treachery."

"There shall be no treachery, sir. You have the word of a German admiral."

"Very well I shall acquaint you with other details from time to time."

This was the conversation that Jack heard that day.

At noon on November 18, Jack, together with other commanders, received word from Admiral Beatty to steam toward Harwich, on the English coast, and to take his place in the long line of ships that would be gathered there to receive the surrender of the enemy fleet.

Excitement thrilled the crew of the Essex. They were about to witness one of the greatest events of world history and there wasn't a man aboard who didn't know it. Nevertheless, there was no confusion, and the Essex steamed rapidly westward.

"Hope we get up near the front of the line," said Frank to his chum. "Also that we are close to Admiral Beatty's flagship."

"Here too," said Jack. "It will be a sight worth seeing."

"Rather."

"Well, we can't kick no matter where they place us, you know. I suppose I shall receive the necessary instructions in plenty of time."

Jack did. The instructions came the following morning, while the Essex was still possibly a hundred miles off the English coast.

"You will report to Admiral Tyrwhitt," Jack's message read, "who will assign you to your station."

Jack immediately got in touch with Admiral Tyrwhitt by wireless. The latter gave his position and informed the lad that his place in line would be next to the Admiral's flagship.

"I thought Admiral Beatty would be up toward the front," said Jack.

"He probably will," was Frank's reply. "I have it figured out like this, from what you have told me of the fact that the submarines will be surrendered first: Admiral Tyrwhitt probably will receive the surrender of the U-Boats, while Admiral Beatty will receive the formal surrender of Admiral von Wimpfen himself."

"Maybe that's it," Jack agreed.

It was well after noon when the Essex sighted the flagship of Admiral Tyrwhitt, the Invincible, and reported for duty. Jack received instructions to lay to just west of the flagship. He obeyed.

From time to time now other vessels appeared and reported to Admiral Tyrwhitt and were assigned places in the long line.

Suddenly there was a cheer from the crews of the many ships. Jack glanced across the water, as did Frank. And then the latter went wild with excitement.

Steaming majestically toward them came five great battleships flying the Stars and Stripes.

"So the Americans will be in at the finish," said Jack.

"You bet they will," declared Frank. "We're always in at the finish."

"Well, you deserve to be this time, I guess," said Jack with a smile.

"We always deserve to be," declared Frank.

"So?" replied Jack. "I'm not going to argue with you about it."

"It wouldn't do any good," declared Frank. "Let me tell you something. If it hadn't been for the United States this war wouldn't be over yet."

"Is that so?" demanded Jack. "Why wouldn't it?"

"Because all the British and French together don't seem to have been able to lick the Germans."

"Rats," exclaimed Jack. "We would have done it in time."

"Maybe so, but there is nothing sure about it It was the Americans who turned the tide at Chateau-Thierry."

"They did some wonderful work, I'm not gain-saying that," Jack admitted. "But I can't see that it was any more remarkable than what the Canadians did at Vimy Ridge."

"Well," said Frank smiling, "while the Canadians are really British subjects, nevertheless they come from the same part of the world as the Yankees. They're made out of the same pattern."

Jack smiled.

"I seem to have spoiled my own argument there, don't I?" he said.

Frank grinned too.

"You've got to admit," he said, "that when the Americans start a thing they go through with it. They never turn back."

"True enough," Jack admitted, "but to my mind it takes them a deuced long time to get started."

"They just want to be sure they're right first," Frank explained.

"Have it your own way. But those five American ships approaching now look mighty good, I'll admit that."

"I never saw a more beautiful sight," declared Frank, and he meant it.

Majestically the American warships steamed along, the leading vessel flying the flag of Admiral Sims. They approached almost to the flagship of Admiral Tyrwhitt and the guns of the two flagships boomed out an exchange of salutes. Then the American flotilla slowed down and swung to leeward, and took its places in the long line.

"Going to be quite an event this surrender, if you ask me," said Frank.

"It certainly is," Jack replied. "I understand King George and Queen Mary, together with many other distinguished British, French, Americans and Italians, will be present to witness the surrender."

"Including ourselves," grinned Frank.

"Well, we're probably not such big fry," Jack commented, "but we've done as much—and a whole lot more—than a good many of them, if you ask me."

"My sentiments exactly," declared Frank. "And for that reason we're just as much entitled to be in at the finish as any of the rest."

"More so," said Jack quietly.

"Well, we'll be there. So we have no kick coming."

All day great vessels of war continued to arrive and take their places in the line. As far as the eye could see long gray shapes lay in the water—two lines of them—with perhaps half a mile between. Through this space the German warships would pass when they came out to surrender.

When the eye could no longer see ships, the presence of other vessels was noted by smudges of smoke on the horizon. The line of ships, or rather the two lines, Jack and Frank knew, stretched almost to the distant shore.

"Yes," said Jack, "it's going to be quite an event."

Suddenly the guns of every ship burst out with a roar. The flagship of Admiral Beatty was approaching down the line from shore.

Aboard it, every man of the great fleet knew, besides the admiral, were King George and Queen Mary of England; and it was the royal salute that was being fired. Even the American ships joined in the greeting.

The guns of Admiral Beatty's flagship were kept busy acknowledging the salutes. On every deck handkerchiefs and caps waved frantically as the flagship passed.

As the vessel drew abreast of the Essex, Jack and Frank, standing together on the bridge, made out the forms of the King and Queen of England on the bridge.

Both lads doffed their caps, and Jack ordered the royal salute fired by the big guns of the destroyer.

The vessel trembled under the detonation and the crew seemed to go wild as they cheered at the top of their voices.

The flagship passed on.

A mile or so to the east, the flagship slowed down and turned into line.

"And that's where I suppose she will remain until after the surrender," said Jack.

The lad was right.

## CHAPTER XXVIII

## THE SURRENDER

Germany's sea surrender began at dawn on November 20, nine days after the signing of the armistice.

Out in this misty expanse of the North Sea the allied battleships had taken up their positions in a fifty-mile line of greyhounds. Aboard the allied battleships every eye was strained to the east; every man was on the alert. The British and allied war vessels presented a noble sight, stretched out as far as the eye could see, and beyond.

Every ship was stripped for action. Crews were at their posts. Not until the surrender was an accomplished fact would the vigilance of the British naval authorities be relaxed. Not until the German vessels were safe in the hands of the allies would British officers and crews be certain that the enemy was not meditating trickery up to the last moment.

The destroyer Essex, commanded by Jack, as has already been said, was at the extreme east of the long line of battleships. Beyond it were the flagship of Admiral Beatty, flanked still farther east by three big war vessels, and Admiral Tyrwhitt's flagship.

Jack and Frank were on the bridge of the destroyer. Other officers were at their posts. The crews stood to their guns. Below, the engine room was the scene of activity. A full head of steam was kept up, for there was no telling at what moment it might be needed.

Came a shrill whistle from the farthest advanced British vessel, followed by a cry from the lookout aboard the destroyer:

"Here they come!"

As the red sun rose above the horizon the first submarine appeared in sight. Soon after seven o'clock, twenty-seven German submarines were seen in line, accompanied by two destroyers. These latter were the Tibania and the Serra Venta, which accompanied the flotilla to take the submarine crews back to Germany.

All submarines were on the surface, with their hatches open and their crews standing on deck. They were flying no flags whatever, and their guns were trained fore and aft in accordance with previous instructions from Admiral Beatty.

Until the moment that they had sighted the first ship of the British fleet, the German flag had flown from the mastheads of the various undersea craft, but they had been hauled down at once when the allied war vessels came into view.

The leading destroyer, in response to a signal from Admiral Beatty on his flagship, altered her course slightly and headed toward the coast of England.

The wireless instrument aboard the destroyer Essex clattered and a few moments later the radio operator rushed to the bridge with a message for Jack. The latter read it quickly, then said:

"Send an O.K. to the admiral?'

"What's up, Jack?" asked Frank.

"Lower half a dozen small boats, Mr. Hetherton," instructed Jack before replying to Frank's question, "and have them manned by a score of men each, fully armed."

"Aye, aye, sir."

Lieutenant Hetherton hurried away.

"What's up, Jack?" asked Frank again.

"I have been ordered to inspect each submarine as it comes abreast of us," Jack replied. "Apparently the admiral still fears treachery. I'll remain aboard here, and leave the work to you and the other officers."

This was done. As each submarine drew up with the Essex she was boarded by a score of the Essex's men. Some stood guard at the hatches with weapons held ready, while an officer and the others of the crew went below for a hurried trip of inspection, searching them diligently for "booby traps," and other signs of treachery.

This necessitated a slowing down in the speed of the German craft, but at length the work was accomplished and Frank and his men, and all others belonging aboard the Essex, returned to their ship.

"All serene, Jack," Frank reported.

"Very well, I shall so inform the admiral."

He scribbled off a brief message, which he sent to the radio room.

Now, with the submarines well along the line, the British fleet began to move—escorting the U-Boats toward Harwich. The fleet would return the next day to receive the surrender of the larger enemy war vessels, but to-day it meant to make sure that the submarines were taken safely to port.

There was one brief halt while the German admiral in command of the flotilla went aboard Admiral Tyrwhitt's flagship to make formal surrender of the submarines. He was accompanied by two members of his staff.

Admiral Tyrwhitt received him on the bridge. There were tears in the eyes of the German admiral as he said:

"Sir, I surrender to you this submarine fleet of the Imperial German navy."

He extended his sword.

Admiral Tyrwhitt waved back the sword and accepted the surrender in a few brief words. The German admiral turned on his heel and walked to the rail. There one of his officers held out his hand to a British lieutenant who was nearby.

The latter refused it, and the German turned away muttering to himself in his native tongue. The German admiral and his officers returned to the destroyer, and the march of the fleets continued.

It was a procession of broken German hopes—in the van, a destroyer of the unbeaten navy; behind, the cruel pirate craft that were to subjugate the sea. Each of the allied warships turned, and keeping a careful lookout, steamed toward Harwich.

As the Essex passed one of the largest submarines, which carried two 5.9 guns, Frank counted forty-three officers and men on her deck. The craft was at least three hundred feet long.

"By George! Isn't she a whopper?" exclaimed the lad.

Jack nodded.

"She is indeed. The largest submarine I ever saw."

Near the Shipwash lightship, three large British seaplanes appeared overhead. They were followed by a single airship. The sight of the Harwich forces, which soon appeared in the distance, together with the seaplanes and the airship, was a most impressive one.

Suddenly two carrier pigeons were released aboard one of the captured submarines.

A shock ran through the officers and crew of every allied vessel in sight. Apparently something was wrong. Sharp orders rang out. But the matter passed over. It was explained that the pigeons had been released merely to carry back to Germany the news that the surrender had been made.

Nevertheless, the act called forth a vigorous protest from the flagship of the British commander-in-chief.

"Another act like that and I shall sink you," was Admiral Beatty's message.

Still ten miles off shore, the procession came to a halt. Feverish activity was manifest aboard the British vessels. Small boats were lowered and put off toward the submarines. These carried British crews that were to take over the vessels and conduct them to port. As fast as a British crew took possession, the German crews were transferred to the German destroyers there for the purpose of taking them back to Germany.

Then the procession moved toward Harwich again.

As the boats went through the gates into Harwich harbor, a white ensign was run up on each of them, with the German flag flying underneath.

Before being removed to the destroyers, which were to carry them back, each submarine commander, who were the only Germans left aboard the vessels as they passed into the harbor, was required to sign a declaration that his submarine was in perfect running order, that his periscope was intact, the torpedoes unloaded and the torpedo head safe.

Despite orders issued to the Harwich forces in advance, to the effect that no demonstration must be permitted in the city after the surrender of the German fleet, wild cheering broke out on the water front as the submarines, escorted by the great British warships, steamed into the harbor.

Military police cleared the water front of the dense throng that had gathered, but the best efforts they put forth were unable to still the bedlam that had broken loose.

Commanders of the British ships had difficulty in restraining cheers by their crews and later by the Harwich forces themselves when the fleet of captured submarines was turned over to Captain Addison, the commandant at that port.

Harbor space for the surrendered U-Boats had been provided in advance, and the vessels were now piloted to these places, where they were placed under heavy guard.

This work took time, and it was almost dark before the last submarine had been escorted to its resting place.

All day crowds thronged the streets of Harwich, cheering and yelling madly. In vain the military authorities tried to stop the celebration. As well have tried to shut out the sound of thunder in the heavens. At last the authorities gave it up as a bad job, and joy and happiness ran rampant and unrestrained.

It was a glorious day for England, and thousands of persons from London and the largest cities of the island had hurried to Harwich to witness the formal surrender of the fleet and its internment. All night the thousands paraded the streets of the little village, the celebration seeming to grow rather than to diminish as the early morning hours approached.

So passed the bulk of Germany's undersea fighting strength into the hands of Great Britain and her allies. No longer would they terrorize with their ruthless warfare. They were safe at last. The fangs of the undersea serpents had been drawn.

And on the night of November 20, 1918, thus made harmless, they lay quietly in the harbor of Harwich, England, above them flying the Union Jack.

## CHAPTER XXIX

## THE SURRENDER COMPLETE

November 21! This was to be a day, perhaps, more historic than the one that preceded it, for on this day was to be surrendered to the allied fleet the bulk of the great war vessels that comprised the Imperial German navy.

Heading the great British flotilla that moved out to sea again was the super-dreadnaught the Queen Elizabeth, Admiral Beatty's flagship, aboard which were King George and Queen Mary, as they had been the day before.

Following the first twenty-five British ships steamed the American squadron, Admiral Rodman, aboard the dreadnaught New York, showing the way. Following the New York were the Florida, Wyoming, Texas and Arkansas. Behind the Americans trailed a pair of French cruisers, followed in turn by a few Italian vessels, after which came the remainder of the great British fleet.

So the flotilla moved out again and took up the positions they had held the day before. Again every eye was strained to catch sight of the first German warship. And at last came the cry, sounding much as it had on the preceding day:

"Here they come!"

The German fleet that approached now came much more swiftly than had the flotilla of undersea craft. This time the halt was made while the German flagship was abreast of the Queen Elizabeth. Admiral Baron von Wimpfen put off for Admiral Beatty's vessel in a launch.

Admiral Beatty received the German admiral on the bridge of the Queen Elizabeth, with him were King George and Queen Mary. Admiral von Wimpfen made the formal declaration of surrender and it was accepted by the British admiral without ostentation.

The German fleet thus turned over to Admiral Beatty consisted of approximately one hundred and fifty vessels of all classes, including dreadnaughts, battleships, cruisers and destroyers. Slowly these giant vessels fell into line now and steamed toward Harwich, the British ships, still cleared for action, accompanying them and watching carefully for the signs of treachery.

But no such signs showed themselves. No longer were the Germans thinking of fight. They had been decisively beaten, and they knew it. Apparently they considered themselves lucky to get off so easily.

Still some distance off-shore, the crews of the German ships were transferred to the half-dozen small vessels that were to carry them back to the Fatherland, and British crews were put aboard the vessels. Then, their eyes sad and watching what had once been the pride of Germany, the German officers and sailors began their cheerless journey home.

Again it was a night of festivity in Harwich, and in all England, and all allied countries, for that matter. The surrender of the great German fleet was now a thing of the past. Germany's hands were tied. She could continue the struggle no longer even should she elect to do so. While a formal declaration of peace had not been signed, and probably would not be signed for months to come, the war was over, so far as actual fighting was concerned.

No wonder England, France, America, Italy and the smaller nations with them went wild with joy. After four years of war, peace had again cast its shadow over the earth, and everyone was glad.

"So it's all over."

It was Frank who spoke. He and Jack were in the latter's cabin on the Essex. The ship was lying at anchor just outside Harwich harbor, riding gently on the swell of the waves.

"Yes, it's all over," said Jack, "and I'm glad."

"So am I," Frank declared; "and yet we have had a good time."

"So we have, of a kind. And still you can't rightly call it a good time when all we have been doing is to seek, kill and destroy."

"But it had to be done," Frank protested.

"Oh, I know that as well as you do. But war is a terrible thing, and the more you see of it the more certain you become that it is all foolishness."

"And yet, you can't permit a big bully to run amuck and smash up things all over the world."

"That's true, of course, and it's exactly what the kaiser and his war machine tried to do. Now, the machine had to be smashed, of course, and it has been smashed. But how long will it take the world to recover? How long will it take to rebuild what has been destroyed in these four years of war?"

Frank shrugged his shoulders.

"I'm not good at conundrums," he replied.

"Nor I; and yet I'll venture to say that the reconstruction days will be as hard as many we have experienced in the war."

"The thing that I want to know," said Frank, changing the subject abruptly, "is just what will be done with Germany in the final peace conference."

"You know as much about it as I do," replied Jack, "but my own idea is that the German empire will be dismembered—divided into the states of Prussia, Saxony, and so forth, as they were years before they united under one head."

"I'm sure I hope so. Certainly the allies will never permit Germany to attain such power that may make all our fighting futile—they'll never let her grow strong enough to start another world struggle."

The lads conversed far into the night before retiring. Nevertheless they were astir at an early hour, awaiting orders that they knew must come that day; and they came shortly after noon in the shape of a wireless from Lord Hastings.

"Return to Dover at once," the message read.

Again the Essex put to sea.

But it was upon a peaceful voyage that the destroyer was bound now. No longer did her decks bristle with shining guns, crew at quarters and ready for action. True, the Essex still showed plainly that she was a ship of war, but her threatening attitude was gone. The war was over and all was quiet aboard.

That night the destroyer put into Dover harbor and the lads went ashore to report to Lord Hastings. It was after ten o'clock, but their former commander received them at once in spite of the lateness of the hour.

"Sorry to disturb you at this hour, sir," said Jack, "but I thought perhaps you would wish us to report to you immediately."

"And I am glad you did," returned Lord Hastings. "Come, tell me something about yourselves. So you were in at the finish, eh?"

"You bet!" exclaimed Frank enthusiastically. "You should have been there, sir."

"I was," replied Lord Hastings.

"You were, sir?"

"Yes."

"But we didn't see you, sir," said Jack.

"I know you didn't. But I saw you. And I saw Frank when he inspected the submarines on the first day of the surrender."

"Where were you, sir?" demanded Frank.

"Aboard the Queen Elizabeth. I viewed the surrender as the guest of Admiral Beatty, and their majesties."

For some time the conversation dealt only with the surrender of the fleet. Then Lord Hastings said:

"Well, boys, the war is over. What do you intend to do now?"

"I know what I shall do, sir," said Frank.

"Well, let's hear it."

"I shall return to America as soon as I am able to procure my discharge."

"As I thought," said Lord Hastings. "And you, Jack?"

"I hardly know, sir. I have no relatives, few friends. There is no one dependent on me, and I am dependent on no one. It strikes me, sir, that the navy might be a good place to stick."

"And I had expected that, too," said Lord Hastings quietly. "But I don't agree with you, Jack."

"Why not, sir?" asked Jack, in some surprise.

"In the first place," said Lord Hastings, "the life would begin to pall on you when it settled down to dull routine. Now in active service, of course, it's different. I know, because I've tried both. No, my advice to you Jack, is to get out of the navy."

"But what shall I do, sir?"

"There are many things," said Lord Hastings quietly. "There is the consular service, the diplomatic service. Who knows how far you may rise? Already you have made a name for yourself and have won distinction. You may go far, if you apply yourself."

"That's true, too, sir," said Jack. "I have thought of that, at odd moments. But I guess you are right about the navy, sir."

"I know I am. And the sooner you get out of it the better."

"Then I'll take your advice, sir. But I'm afraid it won't be possible to get a discharge for some time yet."

"It will be much simpler that you think, for both of you," said Lord Hastings with a smile. "I still have some influence, you know, and I shall see you receive your discharges within a fortnight, if you wish."

"Hurray!" shouted Frank. "That suits me. There is no use sticking in the navy now. There is nothing to do."

"And," continued Lord Hastings to Jack. "In the meantime I'll look around and see what I can turn up for you, Jack."

"Thank you, sir," said Jack.

"And in the meantime, Jack," added Frank, "you are going home with me for a visit. That is, as soon as we get our discharges."

Jack hesitated.

"But I don't know that I should," he said. "Lord Hastings——"

"Go by all means," said Lord Hastings. "You have earned a rest and should take it. Now I'll see about the discharges at once, and as soon as you receive them, both of you take my advice and go to the United States. That will give me additional time to look around, Jack. And when you get there, stay until I send for you."

"All right, sir," said Jack with a smile. "You're still my superior officer, sir. I must obey your commands."

The three shook hands and Jack and Frank returned to the Essex.

## CHAPTER XXX

## HOME AT LAST

"Recognize that, Jack?" asked Frank, pointing across the water.

The lads were standing on the forward deck of a great trans-Atlantic liner that was edging its way into New York harbor.

Jack looked in the direction Frank indicated.

"Rather," he said, "although I only saw it once before. That's the Statue of Liberty."

"Right," said Frank, "the emblem of that for which America went to war."

"And the spirit for which we all fought," Jack added.

"Exactly. Well, it's been a long time since I saw her. I'm glad to see her again."

It was morning of the last day of the year 1918.

True to his word, Lord Hastings had been able to secure discharges for the lads within two weeks after the surrender of the German fleet. They accompanied Lord Hastings to London, where they remained some time at his home. Frank, meanwhile, communicated with his father and announced that he would be home soon. He did not give the exact date, for he wished his return to be a surprise. And a surprise he knew it would be, as he now stood on the deck of the incoming liner.

The ship docked a short time later and Jack and Frank went ashore at once. They took a taxi to the Grand Central station, where they caught a fast train for Boston. It was night when they arrived there, but Frank determined to go out to his home in Woburn, ten miles from Boston, at once.

Accordingly they took an elevated train at the South Station. This put them in the North Station ten minutes later, and Frank found that there was a train for Woburn in half an hour.

It was after dark when the lads alighted from the train in the little town of Woburn. Jack had been there with Frank before, when the lads had crossed the Atlantic to New York soon after the United States entered the war. Accordingly, he knew the way from the station to Frank's home almost as well as the latter did himself.

"Know where you are?" asked Frank.

Jack grinned.

"I've been here once," he said. "That should answer that question. You know my memory is pretty good."

"Then you can show me which house I live in," said Frank.

Jack pointed to a house a block away where a dim light showed from beneath a drawn curtain.

"There's the house," he said, "and there appears to be some one home."

"That's father, of course," said Frank. "He seldom goes out in the evening."

The lads quickened their steps and soon were before the house. Quietly they mounted the steps and as quietly tip-toed across the porch. Frank tried the door. It was unlocked.

"Careless of father," he whispered. "I'll have to speak to him about that."

He opened the door gently and the two lads passed within. Frank closed the door noiselessly behind him. The lads dropped their grips silently in the hall and then tip-toed toward a room at the far end, where a light showed.

Keeping out of sight, Frank peered in the door. There, with his back to his son, sat Dr. Chadwick, reading. Frank stepped softly across the room leaving Jack standing, grinning, at the door.

Frank reached out and put both hands across his father's eyes.

Dr. Chadwick's book dropped to the floor and for a moment Frank was afraid he had frightened him by this unceremonious greeting. But Dr. Chadwick's hands reached up and clasped the hands that for the moment blinded him.

"Frank!" he cried, and sprang to his feet.

The next moment father and son were in each other's arms.

Dr. Chadwick held his son off at arm's length, and looked at him.

"You're a sight for sore eyes," he declared. "You look better than you did the last time I saw you, and you were looking fine then."

"Here, Father," said Frank, "is a friend of mine come to see you."

Dr. Chadwick turned and saw Jack in the doorway. He stepped forward and gripped Jack's hand heartily.

"Jack Templeton, eh?" he exclaimed. "I'm glad to see you. And you are Captain Templeton now, I perceive."

Jack blushed.

"They insisted on making me one, sir, and I couldn't refuse," he said.

"Now," said Dr. Chadwick, "you two boys sit right down here and tell me all about yourselves. But first, are you hungry?"

"No, sir," said Frank. "We had dinner on the train just before we reached Boston."

"Then let's hear what you have been doing. I understand you were present at the surrender of the German fleet. Give me some of the details."

Until long after midnight the three sat there, Dr. Chadwick listening eagerly to the tales of his son and the latter's chum. But at last he looked at his watch.

"Why, it's after midnight," he exclaimed. "Time for bed."

Frank led the way to the room he had occupied since babyhood. This Jack was to share with him during his stay.

"I'll tell you," said Frank, as he climbed into bed, "it feels pretty good to a fellow to get back into his own bed after all these years."

"I should think it would," agreed Jack. "But mine is a long ways from here. However, I guess I shall see it again some day."

"Of course you will, old fellow, and I'll go along with you."

They fell asleep.

Both lads were awakened by the sound of a commotion without. They jumped out of bed. It was broad daylight of the first day of January, 1919.

"Still celebrating the new year, I guess," said Frank. "Remember we heard 'em shooting before we went to bed?"

Jack nodded.

Frank went to the window and stuck his head out. Instantly there was a wild yell outside. Frank drew his head hurriedly back again.

"What's the matter?" asked Jack.

"I don't know," said Frank. "There is a whole gang of fellows out there and they all seem to be crazy about something."

Jack had a faint suspicion. He crossed to the window and looked out.

Again a yell went up, followed by a cry from many throats:

"We want Frank!"

Even Frank heard this. His face turned red and he began to act flustered.

"Some of the fellows know I'm home, I guess," he said.

"That's what's the matter, all right," Jack agreed. "Better show yourself again."

"Wait till I get some clothes on and I'll go down and see 'em," said Frank.

"They'll probably want you to make a speech," Jack suggested.

Frank was alarmed.

"Speech?" he repeated. "I can't make a speech."

"Oh, yes you can. You don't mean to tell me that a fellow who has done what you have—who has talked with kings and czars—is afraid to talk to some of his old friends and companions?"

"That's different," declared Frank.

Jack smiled.

"I catch your point, and maybe you're right," he admitted. "However, you'll have to do it."

"I suppose I shall," said Frank with a sigh, "so the sooner I get it over with the better."

He led the way downstairs and on to the front porch. Jack stepped forward close beside him. Again there was a wild cheer from many throats.

Both lads still wore their British uniforms, and they both presented a manly and handsome appearance as they stood there on the front porch of Frank's home.

"Hello, Frank!" "Glad to see you back!" "Are you going to stay here?" "Tell us about yourself."

These were some of the cries hurled at the lad.

Frank's face turned red and he would have turned away had not Jack's stalwart frame stayed him.

"Speech! Speech!" came the cry.

The hubbub increased.

"I can't do it, Jack!" Frank exclaimed.

"Oh, yes you can," replied his chum. "I'll help you."

He raised his right hand for silence, still keeping his left tightly on Frank's shoulder, for the latter showed signs of bolting at the first opportunity. Instantly the shouting died away and the crowd of young fellows waited expectantly.

"I just want to introduce my friend," said Jack smiling. "Lieutenant Chadwick, gentlemen, of His British Majesty's service, though an American citizen, and a good one at that. Lieutenant Chadwick will be glad to say a few words to you."

The cheering burst forth again, but died away as Jack pushed Frank forward.

Frank made a brave effort and finally managed to say a few words. He grew more at ease as he went along and his audience listened intently. He spoke for perhaps five minutes, then concluded:

"And now, fellows, I want you all to step up and shake hands with my friend—also my commander—Captain Jack Templeton. He's an Englishman, but a pretty good fellow at that—and he's no older than any of us."

There was another cheer and the boys gathered around to shake Jack's hand and get acquainted with him. And after they had talked and talked and feasted their eyes on the British uniforms to their hearts' content they went away. Then Jack and Frank went in to breakfast, where Dr. Chadwick was awaiting them at the table.

A few words more and the history of The Boy Allies on the Sea is complete.

Jack remained with Frank for several weeks, then returned to England upon receipt of a message from Lord Hastings announcing that he had found a place for the lad in the diplomatic service. The story of Jack's struggles in his chosen profession would make interesting reading, perhaps, but it is in no wise connected with the great war. Suffice it to say that he is rapidly rising to fame and fortune and that in years to come, in all probability, he will hold one of the most important posts in the British government.

Frank, for his part, remained in his home town, where he took up the study of law. He proved an apt student and soon showed signs of talent that undoubtedly will make him famous.

So here we shall take our leave of Jack Templeton and Frank Chadwick, knowing that, in years to come, they will meet again, both famous then, and that through all the years their friendship shall survive, and grow stronger than it was in the days when they fought side by side for the freedom of the world.

THE END

Lightning Source UK Ltd.
Milton Keynes UK
UKHW010627080121
376670UK00001B/207